Woo Me

BOOK 2 OF THE OUTBACK BACHELOR BALL SERIES

KARINA BLISS

Woo Me
Copyright: 2015 Karina Bliss
ISBN: 9780994116543
e-ISBN: 9780994116536

Cover design: Out of House Creative
Story editor: Wanda Ottewell
Proofreader: Jane Madison-Jones
Formatter: AuthorEMS

Many thanks to adviser Sharyn Barratt and my beta readers – Janine, Kaetrin and Keely.

And to Joan Kilby and Sarah Mayberry for inviting me on this great adventure!

The Outback Bachelor Ball series*

A cow, a cowgirl and a divorcee walk into a bar...

Three unlucky-in-love girlfriends make a road trip to the
Outback Bachelor & Spinster Ball, a highlight of rural
Australian life. One's looking to move on, one's
thumbing her nose at romance, and one's looking to slip
away and hide. None of them are looking for love...
Three women are about to meet their match in a cowboy,
a soldier and a country rock star.
One magical night.
One less than magical morning after.
Forty-eight hours can change your life.

WIN ME by Joan Kilby
Book 1

WOO ME by Karina Bliss
Book 2

WAIT FOR ME by Sarah Mayberry
Book 3

* The events in all three novellas happen concurrently.
They don't have to be read in order to avoid spoilers, but
we think the order suggested above offers readers the
best experience. To read excerpts of the other novellas
visit www.joankilby.com and www.sarahmayberry.com

Author's Note

The life of a writer is a solitary one. So when Aussie authors Sarah Mayberry and Joan Kilby emailed to ask if I wanted to work on a fun joint project of three novellas the first thing I did was ~~change out of my trackpants, get off social media, straighten my posture~~ say, Let me check my diary. That took about three seconds.

These authors are auto-buys for me and it's been an honor to brainstorm heroines and stories with them. The world we created together has become as real to me as the one I live in. I hope you enjoy reading the adventures of Ellie, Jen and Beth.

Joan, Karina and Sarah sure had a lot of fun writing them.

Woo Me

CHAPTER 1

"I'D GIVE YOU A GOOD reference," Karl said. The general manager at the Noosa Beachbreak Hotel and Conference Center—tall, fair and affable—smiled. Briefly, Jen Tremaine imagined her fist slamming through her boyfriend's chemically-whitened teeth.

Ex-boyfriend. Last night, Karl had dropped the bombshell that he'd fallen in love with his ex-wife. Her emotions still raw, the harsh rejoinder trembled on the tip of her tongue—*A good reference for being what, a sucker?* But she was determined to be in control of this.

"Why would I resign?" she said instead, ignoring all the other churning whys. Why didn't you know your own mind? Why didn't I see this coming? Why aren't you acknowledging my anguish with some real regret?

Perhaps her face revealed those thoughts. Karl's gaze shifted to her office window where the Queensland sun set over the Noosa River in a brassy blaze of glory. Jen had been sitting at her desk, working late when he'd walked in. For a breathless moment she'd expected him to say it had all been a bad joke.

Karl cleared his throat. "I think it will be uncomfortable continuing to work together."

Thank God she'd learned young how to quarantine her feelings. That survival skill was the only thing keeping Karl alive. "When you were first chasing me for a date," she reminded him quietly, "you stressed your ability to separate your personal and professional lives."

She resisted the urge to glance at the open diary on her desk, where their first anniversary was highlighted. She'd already booked the restaurant. "But if you want to ask for a transfer to another hotel," she added, "you go ahead."

Karl looked back at her, frowning, and she held his gaze. She loved her job as conference manager, loved her team and this was his mess, not hers. It wouldn't be easy but she'd weathered worse in her twenty-eight years.

"You can work with a guy who dumped you?" he countered.

"I can work with a guy who mistook his feelings," Jen was proud of the steadiness of her voice. "And is respectful of mine."

Karl reddened. "I'm sorry. That was a shitty thing to say." He started to pace. "I can't help how I feel about Sally, Jen."

"I get that," she said desperately. Please don't tell me again how you've realized your ex is everything you ever wanted in a woman. His pacing was flattening the pile in the long weave rug. He could have been a predator trailing through the long grass toward his next kill. Oh God, this hurt. "But you can help how I feel by not making a bad situation worse."

"Hey, I wasn't the one who insisted on telling head office we'd begun a relationship."

"Because I wanted everything open and above board. No sneaking around, no conflicts of interest." Her watch pinged a reminder to link into Skype on her laptop. Her stomach plummeting on a horrifying thought Jen ignored it. "Karl, you and Sally haven't been sleeping together while we've been dating..." Her voice cracked. "Have you?"

He stopped pacing to look out the window again, the sunset an orange halo around his blonde head. "You know how this is going to play at HQ, don't you? I'll be the bad guy and you'll be the victim."

Jen winced at the vocalization of her worst nightmare. "Not if we keep the breakup civil," she insisted, more for her sake than his. "Professional." She bit her tongue to stop herself repeating her earlier question. Had he and Sally…?

"There's another reason." Karl turned. "Sally's not comfortable with us working together."

There was an ornamental paper knife in Jen's in-tray. Her fingers itched for it. She held onto her self-control through sheer force of will. "That's not my problem, Karl. I love this job, I'm not resigning because you didn't know your own heart."

How did we even come to this? He'd been separated six months when Jen joined the hotel and they'd worked well together, her detail-focused personality a good foil for the general manager's expansive charm. She'd said no when Karl first suggested a date. Instead she'd waited until the dust settled on his divorce, waited until he'd worked through his rebound flings, waited until he'd stopped referencing his ex-wife. Dammit, I did everything possible to keep myself safe.

"Now if you'll excuse me," Jen re-focused on her laptop. "I have a call with Beth and Ellie scheduled." Her two besties had anchored her life since boarding school and their monthly Skype catch-up waited for no man.

Karl frowned at the dismissal, but walked toward the door. "We'll talk about this again."

"You won't change my decision." Not looking at him, she cleared her screensaver and searched for the Skype icon.

But after Karl had left and her margarita arrived from the hotel bar—a cocktail was part of the friends' ritual—

Jen had to scull half of the sour-sweet liquor before her hands stopped trembling enough to click the link. If she discussed the breakup she'd cry—so she wouldn't discuss it.

"Hey, Jen, are you there?" Ellie McFarlane came into focus, sitting in her bunkhouse. She worked on a ranch in Wyoming cattle country and wore a faded plaid shirt. "Can you see me?" In one hand she clutched her jam jar glass of margarita, with the other she tried to neaten her sun-streaked brown ponytail.

"I'm here." Jen's forced smile eased seeing Ellie's token attempt at grooming. Thank God, some things never changed. "Beth's not online yet," she added. "Is she coming?"

They were both crazy anxious about their other bestie since her marriage had imploded a month earlier.

"Hope so," Ellie said, giving up on the ponytail. "Though I wouldn't blame Beth if she curled up under the covers for the next year." She scowled. "Have you seen the news reports of that asshat husband of hers?"

"How could I miss?" Jen said grimly. Beth Walker had married a country music star and the world's press was having a field day reporting his infidelities.

"I wish we could be with her," Ellie said. She needs us. I guess you're busy with work, and with Karl, but it would be great if we could meet up somewhere."

Jen squirmed at the reference to Karl but before she could answer, Beth appeared on the split screen. "Hey, Ellie, Jen."

Jen forgot her own troubles. Seated on a rumpled bed, Beth held a mini-bar-sized tequila bottle and looked heartrendingly vulnerable, blonde hair slashed into a pixie cut that highlighted her delicate bone structure and sad, brown eyes. She'd lost weight in the last month—a lot of it.

"Sweetie." Ellie's tone echoed the dismay Jen was feeling. "Where are you?"

"I'm in some god-forsaken dot on the map." Beth shrugged thin shoulders. "I don't even know if it's Oklahoma or Texas. I just needed to get away from the paparazzi."

"How are you holding up?" said Jen softly.

"I'm great now that I'm talking to you two." Beth lifted her miniature tequila bottle. "My first toast of the night—I propose we send all country and western singers in the universe to the darkest pit of hell."

"That's the spirit," Jen encouraged, raising her drink. If Beth wanted to rage, then rage they would. "Some men aren't worth the trouble." The reminder steadied her own resolve. Karl is not going to pressure me into resigning. He can transfer if he wants to.

"Down with all dickheads." Ellie said and drank with relish.

"Does that mean you've given up on that boneheaded cowboy of yours?" Beth asked. "About time if you ask me. He's a fool not to appreciate the gorgeous woman in his own backyard."

"I haven't been around Rick in six years," Ellie said with a hint of defensiveness. "But no, I doubt anything's changed." Jen exchanged speaking looks with Beth. The wistfulness in their friend's eyes suggested her feelings hadn't changed either. Ellie had been in love with the manager of her family's cattle station in Aussie for as long as Jen could remember. And he treated her like his kid sister.

"I think I'm going to come back to Australia," Beth blurted. Her expression suggested she was as surprised as they were and Jen rushed in with positive reinforcement.

"A change of scenery will do you wonders." Come home, poor baby, I'll look after you. "Book into a spa for a week. I'll come, too." Taking leave isn't running away, she told herself, it's regrouping. It would give the gossip time to die down and help her and Karl to transition into an entirely professional relationship.

Ellie whooped. "If you two are getting together, then count me in."

"Seriously?" Beth said.

"I'll quit my job," Ellie said decisively. "We'll have a reunion."

Jen's bruised spirits leapt. This was better than she could have hoped for. Her sisters-of-the-heart, all together again.

"Yes! Yes, times a thousand." Beth smiled through tears as she repeated their teenage mantra, no longer trying to be brave. Jen ached for her.

"I have news too." She couldn't keep a secret from her besties. "Karl and I broke up." Saying it for the first time stabbed her with sadness. "It's complicated and I can't talk about it right now, if you don't mind." She tried to smile, couldn't, so settled for a weak joke. "I need more than one margarita for that."

"Shit, Jen, I'm so sorry." Beth touched the screen. "We can cry in our beer together."

"No crying." Jen blinked furiously. "Some men aren't worth the trouble, remember?"

"We should do something special," said Ellie, chewing thoughtfully on her bottom lip.

Uh-oh, Ellie only did that when she was brewing misch-

"Oh, I know!" Ellie's ponytail swung as she bounced on her bunk. "There's a Bachelor and Spinster ball in Dubbo next month."

Jen's spirits rose. Her friends had always been able to talk her into escapades. "An Outback Ball, why not?" The events were a feature of rural Australian life, a chance for isolated country singletons to dance, drink and hopefully find love. "Us, all together again. We'll have a reunion weekend to end all weekends."

She badly needed these women right now, they reminded her that she was strong.

"Fast food, fast talking, fast men." Ellie's green eyes

had a demonic sparkle. "It'll start a new chapter for all of us."

"I'm in for everything but the fast men," Beth said, raw pain in her voice. She caught Jen and Ellie exchanging worried glances. "Only nice guys in the future."

"Take it from me, nice guys are overrated," Ellie said bitterly, clearly thinking of her cowboy again.

"Who wouldn't want you, Ellie?" Jen said. She was so sick of the stupid men in their lives. "You're this gorgeous, adventurous derring-do kind of gal. I'm coming back as you in my next life... Except maybe with more interest in fashion."

"I don't know why you would say that." Grinning, Ellie smoothed down her plaid shirt, pausing to rub a smudge of grease.

"But I'm with Beth," Jen added. Might as well get this out there now. "Count me out on men, nice or otherwise. I'm on a break." Probably permanent. She concentrated on fishing the umbrella out of her margarita until she'd got her emotions under control. "Maybe I'll become a lesbian," she deadpanned. "Either of you keen?"

"As long as there's no sex," said Ellie.

Jen grinned. "Deal." Her grin faded. Come to think of it, sex with Karl had been tepid the last couple of months. She should have read the signs earlier.

"Did you love him very much?" Warm, empathetic Beth always asked the hard questions.

Jen shifted in her chair. "I didn't love Karl in the 'truly madly, deeply' kind of way. I never do fall in love like that. So I'll get over him." Whether she'd trust men again... "What's more important to Ellie and I," she added firmly, "is making sure Troy isn't leaving you with permanent scars, Beth." She glanced at Ellie and received an emphatic nod.

"Is Troy—" Ellie asked Beth who cut her off with a tense smile.

"I don't want to talk about Troy. Let's make our reunion weekend a bastard-free zone. It's about the be-atches y'all."

Beth fist-pumped the air making Jen and Ellie laugh. Their girl was down, but not out.

As they finalized details of their upcoming reunion Jen couldn't believe how much better she felt around her girlfriends. The grief, hurt and humiliation over Karl still festered, but its vise-like intensity had eased under shared laughter. I can get through this.

"Costumes optional," Ellie said and Jen giggled.

"Didn't you wear a cow suit to an Outback ball after high school graduation? That was wrong on so many levels."

Ellie stuck her nose in the air. "I'll have you know Clarabelle was every inch a lady."

"You can't wear it this time," Beth said firmly. "No more hiding your light under a bushel."

"I guess," said Ellie.

Jen heard the doubt. An intervention was clearly required.

"If you still have it, I'll wear the cow suit," she said recklessly. "It'll be my feminist protest against the meat market connotations."

"You're all talk, Jen," said Ellie. "You'll change your mind sober."

"Won't."

"Will."

"Might."

"Dare you," Beth interjected.

"Double dare," Ellie seconded. "You can't refuse a double dare, Jen."

"We made that rule up when we were fourteen," Jen protested. "We're grownups now."

"And look how well that turned out," said Beth, sending them into gales of laughter.

"Fine, I accept the dare." Noisily, Jen sucked the last

of her margarita through the straw and slammed the empty glass on her desk. "Long as everyone's in. Ellie, you have to let Beth and I style you for this ball. Let's show that wooden-skulled cowboy you're all growed up." She snorted. "Except when we're together."

"And Beth..." Ellie looked thoughtful. "Castrate your ex along with the bulls?"

Beth pulled a face. "Too gory even if he deserves it."

"No cowering," Jen said. "No wallflowering. No slinking around avoiding attention." Maybe she should always brainstorm on margaritas. "Any guy who asks you to dance—anyone who isn't a creep or a drunkard, that is—you say yes to."

CHAPTER 2

TWO WEEKS LATER, JEN HAD never needed her friends so badly.

Skulking in her office, listening to the muted laughter of her colleagues in the adjoining boardroom, she opened Skype on her laptop, praying Ellie was online now she'd returned to Australia. A vain hope. Ranchers didn't work social hours.

Closing her eyes, she mentally teleported to the Outback station in New South Wales wishing she was alongside her friend, checking stock or repairing a fence. Hell, even castrating a bull would be better than this.

Jen didn't consider phoning Beth; her other bestie had enough shit to deal with. Thirty-four women—and climbing—had claimed affairs with Beth's husband. Though together, Jen and Beth could have bitched about what asshats men were. *Some* men. Even in the midst of a major case of avoidance and her first panic attack, Jen struggled to be reasonable…fair.

"Ask Jen," everyone said. "She has her head screwed on." Resting her elbows on her desk, she propped that screwed head in her hands now and bit her lip. Her Kiwi half was arguing against making a scene while her Aussie half insisted she "quit cowering and get out there. This hotel is *your* turf!" Besides, the staff were celebrating a success that was predominantly hers. The hotel had won a Conference Venue of the Year award under her leadership.

Another burst of laughter. She couldn't hide here much longer. Her colleagues would feel sorry for her and they'd only just stopped. Jen rubbed her eyes, exhausted. Repressing the grief of her breakup with Karl—at least in public—had been harder than she'd expected. But she'd been winning until now.

Was Karl trying to *embarrass* her into resigning? Why else would the hotel manager invite his ex-wife, Sally, to a work function two weeks after dumping Jen?

Buying herself another couple of minutes, she shuffled items on her immaculate desk and her ticket to the Bachelor and Spinster Ball fell to the floor. As she returned it to its envelope she glanced at Ellie's accompanying note. *You can't refuse a double dare!*

Maybe her way out of this room was treating her impasse with Karl like a double dare challenge? Reaching for her handbag, Jen forced herself to freshen her make-up, pretending her lipstick was war paint.

She could forgive Karl for falling back in love with his ex-wife but she couldn't forgive him for rubbing salt into the wound by inviting Sally to this work function. He could have left Jen with a little dignity.

In the compact's mirror she saw a tear roll down her cheek and ruthlessly flicked it away with her make-up brush before covering the traces with powder. She'd thought she and Karl had been friends as well as lovers. Guess she'd thought wrong.

Jen snapped her compact shut and let fear and pride propel her to the door—fear of being thought needy and pride in her reputation for having a cool head.

Pinning a serene smile on her face, she strolled into the adjacent boardroom. Judging by the half-dozen empty champagne bottles and the raucous level of conversation, celebratory drinks were well underway.

Even Bob from accounts had loosened his tie and several of Jen's female colleagues had kicked off their heels to release cramped toes. Just a family party, she told herself, twenty conference, catering and hospitality staff enjoying a rare relaxing of standards.

A quick scan ascertained that Karl was nowhere in sight. *Perfect*. Returning greetings, Jen grabbed a flute of champagne from the sideboard and headed directly for his ex-wife. Sally watched her approach with the trepidation of a woman who knew she'd won an unreliable happiness.

"Hi, Sal, I wanted to come say hello." With a warm smile, Jen offered her hand to the dainty blond. They'd met several times over the previous year, through pick-ups of the couple's two kids and had a civil relationship. Contrary to what Sal feared, that didn't have to change.

After a brief hesitation, the other woman took her hand. "Hello, Jen."

The buzz of conversation lowered a decibel as bystanders strained to listen without appearing to.

Jen lowered her voice. "I realize this is awkward, but we can get past it."

Relief smoothed the other woman's features, and something else, an odd triumph. Her fingers tightened briefly. "I'm so glad you feel that way."

She lifted her left hand to smooth her hair and Jen caught the glint of a big diamond, clustered by sapphires. Shiny and new. For a split second her smile wobbled like jelly before she steadied it. "Congratulations," she croaked. "I hope you'll be very happy second time around."

"Karl said you knew…" Reluctant sympathy entered the other woman's blue eyes.

"Hey, we're all grownups here." Still smiling, Jen turned away blindly and joined the first cluster of people she stumbled into, making sure she added to the chatter and cheer. Making sure no-one guessed how much she was hurting. But there was a cold hard core of anger, too. *That bastard will* not *make me resign.*

A few minutes later, Karl entered the boardroom, all confidence and charm, his height distinguishing him from the crowd. His gaze met Jen's, assessing. She lifted her chin and mouthed, "Nice try."

Affecting innocence, his attention moved to Sally. As he weaved through the throng toward his new fiancée, Jen glimpsed his kids, Nico and Caitlin, trotting alongside. Spotting his mother, Nico dropped his daddy's hand and ran to Sally's side, where he peeped out shyly from behind her skirt. The three-year-old caught sight of Jen, his eyes lit up and he waved.

Jen waved back, her throat tightening. They'd spent some time together at parks and zoos and were friends. Whatever Karl's faults, he was a good dad. Jen had hoped that maybe one day she and Karl might…

Caitlin turned to see who her little brother was waving at and saw Jen. Across her small face skittered all the emotions the adults were hiding. Confusion, hostility, sadness, apprehension. The five-year-old edged closer to her father.

For a long moment, Jen froze, paralyzed by déjà vu— she knew exactly how it felt to be a child looking for sanctuary. *I'm wrong, we're not all grownups here.*

She plonked her full champagne flute on the nearest surface, politely excused herself, and slipped away to her office. Shutting the door behind her, she leaned against it and pressed her knuckles into her eyelids until she knew she wouldn't cry. *A child's interests should always come first.*

At her desk, she dropped into her chair, opened a new document on her laptop and began to type.

Please accept this letter as my two-weeks' notice of resignation.

"It's tragic," Ellie said, dumping her wine-glass on the clumpy grass at the makeshift camping ground in Dubbo. "The first time in years we're finally living in the same country and you're leaving for New Zealand tomorrow." The canvas chair creaked as she reached for the mallet, her gaze on a wobbly tent peg. "Tell me again why you couldn't have gotten another job in Australia?"

"Because a job came up in Auckland," Jen said. *Where the chances of running into Karl professionally are slim.* Confiscating the mallet, she tossed it aside and applied the last false nail to the pinkie on Ellie's right hand. "No manual labor until the glue dries, remember?"

Beth stood behind Ellie styling their friend's tangle of golden-brown hair for the Bachelor and Spinster Ball at the adjacent showgrounds. "And you really, *really* can't delay your departure for a few more days?" she said. Pausing to take a sip of her Sauvignon, she grinned at Jen, her brown eyes reflecting their shared delight in being together again.

They sat in the meager shade afforded by the canopy of their three-woman domed tent, drinking wine and eating the canapés artfully arranged on the cooler lid.

"I really, *really* can't." A former employer—The Grand Hotel—had offered Jen a three-month contract within hours of the jungle drums telegraphing her resignation. "Like I said, the existing conference co-ordinator has taken emergency leave and there's a major event on Wednesday."

Jen would have to hit the ground running, which would leave her no time to mope. Perfect. "My new boss wanted me yesterday but no way was I missing this weekend, even if it means wearing that damn cow suit."

Packing up her nail kit, she gently toed Clarabelle who sprawled like a comic rug between the tent and Ellie's battered ute with an expression of permanent surprise. The Holstein onesie was made of polyester fleece, the furry white hide dappled with large black blobs. A pink udder with a zipper acted as a back-to-front fanny pack.

Ellie, who'd stretched out her hand to catch the late afternoon sun and was admiring the glints of gold in her painted nails, gave an unladylike snort. "I can't wait to see you in this." Ducking Beth's ministrations, she hauled Clarabelle's head onto her lap and patted her wistfully. "We had good times, didn't we, girl?"

"Don't even think about reneging on your part of the dare, missy," said Beth, her blond pixieness belied by the steely glint in her eye. "You're going glamorous and gorgeous and that's final."

Confiscating Clarabelle, Beth lobbed her head to Jen, who caught it deftly and placed it on the ute tray that held their open suitcases. Clarabelle's large glassy eyes rolled like pinballs with any movement. Her left eye was encircled by another black marking which, depending on your point of view, lent Clarabelle a jaunty pirate-with-eye patch vibe or made her look the sad loser of a bar brawl.

The wild tuft between her horns suggested a bad forelock day and matched the one at the end of her tail. She was endearing and ugly and Jen thanked God no one would recognize her under it.

Beth pulled Ellie's hair into a topknot. "What do you think, Jen? Up or down?"

"Definitely down." Patting Clarabelle's soft pink muzzle, Jen refocused on the makeover. "I have a battery-operated hair straightener somewhere." She retrieved it from her open suitcase.

"So *that's* what that sausage-shaped bag holds," Beth deadpanned. "I did *wonder* when I saw it in the bathroom last night."

They all got the giggles then. It was always like this when they got together, lots of sass and silliness and fun. Jen had met them at the darkest time of her life. She'd been sent to Woodhill Girls' boarding school at the age of twelve in a misguided attempt by her parents to protect her from the fallout of their acrimonious divorce.

Her Australian mother had loved the place during her childhood; shy and shell-shocked, it had felt like exile to New Zealand-raised Jen until Ellie had taken her under her wing. Beth had arrived two years later and the sisterhood was complete.

"Ouch." Ellie winced as a strand of hair snagged in the straightener. "Being beautiful is hard work."

Her friend had seen Rick on arrival at the campground—the station manager Ellie had a crush on since forever—and his unexpected attendance had unsettled her. Not that Ellie would admit that.

Stoic, fearless and practical, the only area in which she lacked confidence was her femininity. Jen thought she'd wasted too many years waiting for Rick to notice she was a woman. Well, tonight Ellie would have her pick of cowboys because her friends were transforming her into the sexiest woman at the ball.

"The man stampede will be worth it," Beth soothed. "I promise."

Jen watched Beth work her magic on Ellie's hair with the straightener, leaving it silky and shiny. It was good to give Beth a project, a distraction. That's what this weekend was all about, reminding Beth there was another world beyond the desert of her divorce. And that world held friends and laughter, excitement and a few good men. Resigned to her own heartbreak, Jen hated seeing her once-buoyant friend so sad.

She'd never understood the blind loyalty Beth had given to Troy; or the years Ellie had wasted pining for Rick. Jen always said flippantly that she approached love like swimming—staying in the shallow end. But the breakup with Karl had left her straining on tippy-toes, barely keeping her head above water.

Feeling tension creep into her neck, she consciously relaxed her shoulders and topped up everyone's wine. She came from a broken home and infidelity had shattered Beth's marriage. Embroiling herself in a love triangle—even inadvertently—left Jen feeling ashamed. Of being so wrong about a guy, of the messiness of it all, of her uncharacteristic lack of judgment.

Her innate caution meant she didn't make mistakes often, and in her romantic life never.

"You okay, Jen?" Ellie asked quietly. Beth lowered the straightener.

"Just considering what slutty lipstick to pick for you," she lied cheerfully. They were here to play, and remind each other they were strong, resilient women, in charge of their own destinies. "Don't smirk, Beth. You're dancing with every half-decent guy who asks you, remember?"

"You don't cow me," Beth taunted.

"Ooh, ooh, I have her theme song," Ellie said. "'Mooooves like Jagger.'" She and Beth laughed.

Jen grinned. Recklessness flickered to life, the way it always did around her best buds. "Works for me," she said. Draping Clarabelle's lifeless hide over her body she did some hip thrusts, watched as her friends convulsed with laughter. *I like who I am with these women. Looser, more fun. Adventurous even.*

It was freeing not to take part in the getting-gorgeous preparations. A relief not putting her best face forward, the glossy, perfect facade that was both her trademark and security blanket.

"I love you guys," she blurted, taking all of them by surprise. Hmph, she'd also been free to drink most of the wine. "You know that, don't you?"

Both women glanced at her empty glass and grinned. "We love you too, babe," Beth said, "but you're *still* wearing that cow suit."

Not for the first time since he'd resigned his commission, Logan Turner wondered if it would have been easier to stay in Special Forces than re-bond with his family. Hell, he had more confidence handling explosives than he did his little sister.

"I know it's a last-minute thing." Lily threw him the beseeching-puppy, my-hero combo he recognized from childhood. "But the security firm was expensive so we beefed up numbers with volunteers and some are a bit use—" She coughed. "I mean *new*. If you could help out for a couple of hours...tell them how to act at the gate, how to patrol boundaries, that sort of stuff."

She even had the princess-in-distress look going, pink satin ball gown, sparkly shoes and an up-do with blond tendrils. "I feel terrible, but we need a professional to lend some guidance and add extra muscle." Lily batted the family's baby-blues at him. "It won't be for long."

"Uh-huh," Logan said skeptically.

From previous leaves, he knew how this would go. Two hours would stretch to three. A crisis would flare and he'd step in because Logan's training and his character made it impossible not to. There could not be two siblings less alike than he and his 'it'll all work out with fairy dust and positive thoughts' sis.

Lily registered his lack of enthusiasm. "What else will you do?" she wheedled. "As one of the organizers I'll be too busy to hang out with you."

"I've been surrounded by guys for nine months. Maybe I want to meet a pretty woman."

"Think how many you'll meet at the gate."

"I'm sure I can make a big impression in the thirty seconds I'm checking their passes," he said dryly.

Checking her clipboard, Lily patted his arm. "You're a honey."

"I mean, look at the impression I'm making on you," Logan added, but she was already gliding away to her next task, all rustling satin and selective hearing.

"What did I hire this monkey suit for again?" he called. Lily laughed and kept walking. "Because I'm a monkey," he muttered, then hollered after his sister. "Two hours only. I'm setting my watch."

And she was gone.

Logan tugged off his bow tie, tucked it in his jacket pocket and unbuttoned the top buttons of the starched shirt. Passing the bar with a regretful sigh, he headed toward the security tent to introduce himself.

There he found an enthusiastic welcome and a bunch of security volunteers ranging in age from sixteen to seventy, being organized into teams by the five professionals his tight-fisted sister and her organizing committee had deigned to pay for.

The pros fell on him like manna from heaven and within ten minutes he found himself with his own security detail.

"How many tickets did they sell to this thing?" he asked Tim, the guy in charge, as he gave Logan a security tag and fluorescent orange armband.

"Six hundred."

Logan did the math. One security guard per sixty people inside a fenced 2,500 square meter area. Easy until you factored in drunkenness and wild country spirits. "Work harder, play hardest" was a creed invented by the farming community. The event was centered on a tent pavilion but from personal experience, Logan knew trouble would come from peripheral areas.

"You a B&S virgin?" Tim asked as he showed Logan around. Inside the pavilion, a plywood floor had been laid over grass. A bar and seating filled one half, a stage and dance floor the other.

"No, mate, but I haven't been to one of these balls since I was seventeen." Sixteen years ago.

He could see his sister's hand in the décor. Fairy lights festooned the walls, high enough, he noted approvingly, not to be dragged down by drunken revelers. The white tablecloths were paper, and some artist—Lily?—had drawn colorful doilies in lieu of a centerpiece. Any damage here would be minimal.

They walked outside. The air was dry, hot with the sizzle of beef and lamb roasting on spits and the rich yeastiness of beer and Bundaberg rum. Logan breathed it all in. Home. It had been a month since he'd resigned from the Australian Army and he felt like a teenager, with his future wide open with possibilities.

On either side of the pavilion entrance, open-sided tents—for food and beverages, first aid, lost and found, and reception—created a central piazza. Lines of portable toilets had been positioned at a discreet distance behind the tents. Semi-trailers carrying catering supplies and band equipment parked a hundred and fifty meters from the main thoroughfare. Logan tallied distances, noting the lighting placement, and where the shadows would fall come dark.

"Steer anyone thinking of driving home tonight to the first aid tent," Tim advised. "The organizers are offering voluntary breath tests. They're also providing subsidized breakfasts tomorrow to help mop up all the alcohol."

Go, Lily. His baby sister *had* grown into a sense of responsibility.

"And there's a dude in a rabbit costume giving out free condoms," Tim added.

Logan grinned. Interpreted in Lily's own whimsical way.

A seven-foot-high chain link security fence separated the ball grounds from the public campground, where tents were sprouting like mushrooms. He spotted bushman's swags and several double mattresses slung into ute trays as well as luxury campers and conventional tents. Party-goers traveled up to six hundred kilometers to these events, and you could see every mile in the dust on their vehicles.

Four young guys in ill-fitting tuxedos stood around their campsite, country rock blaring from unseen speakers. A beer keg took pride of place in the passenger seat of their battered Land Rover. As Logan watched, they toasted each other with brimming schooners of foaming beer. Stoking up on false courage. He'd been a shy country boy himself once, stuttering and blushing in front of a pretty girl. *Good luck, boys*.

He made a mental note to keep an eye on them as Tim spelled out the rules. "No BYO alcohol permitted into the B&S arena. No glass. Food dye is confiscated. There's a ban on car roof surfing and circle work—that's spinning your vehicle in tighter and tighter circles."

"I'm familiar with circle work." Logan tried not to smile. Hopefully, these kids wouldn't get into half the trouble he had.

"The arena's on lockout from nine," Tim said. "Until then punters can leave and re-enter if they get a pass."

By the time the security chief had walked Logan through potential trouble spots, dusk was falling and the party-goers were beginning to arrive. Some of the guys wore Akubra's—battered and sweat-stained—with their suits, while many of the women, elegant and fragrant in stunning evening dresses, sported work boots, the terrain being too rutted and dusty for stilettos. More's the pity, Logan thought, enjoying being around the feminine again.

A cow wandered into sight arm-in-arm with two gorgeous women and he frowned. "I thought black tie was mandatory?" At least that's what Lily had told him when she'd forced him to rent a monkey suit.

"Look closer," Tim invited.

Logan dragged his appreciative gaze from the beauties. *Damn you, Lily, one of them could have been my future bride*. The crazy-eyed Holstein wore a bow tie.

"There's always some clown who has to bend the rules," Tim commented. "We let 'em in so long as they're reasonably sober and the costume is G-rated."

"G-rated?"

Tim grinned. "Underpants under the togas."

The cow paused to hitch up its middle and adjust its head. Warm night, furry suit, the guy clearly hadn't thought this through. On the other hand, he escorted two very pretty women so who was really the idiot here?

Logan looked at his watch and made a note of the time. One and a half hours to go.

CHAPTER 3

JEN BALANCED ON THE BAR stool, tail draped over her knees to discourage tugging and tried to find Clarabelle's mouth with a straw. She was discovering all kinds of drawbacks to this outfit.

The barman leaned forward to help. "Let me."

"Thanks." The straw finally hit her teeth and she sucked up the iced water gratefully. It had been a long hot walk between their tent and the venue. Thirty minutes in and she was already itchy and sweaty.

"You're brave wearing that," he commented. The bar staff were menacingly chic, dressed head to toe in black—jeans, T-shirt, apron and hat—but this one had tilted his Akubra, which gave him an aw-shucks friendliness.

Clumsily, Jen removed the straw with her hoof mitten. "I thought more people would be in costume." At least no one could see how humiliated she was.

"I meant once these cowboys get drunk, you might find yourself a target."

"Oh." She'd smack her forehead if she could get past the padding. "Never accept a dare on an empty stomach and a margarita," she said ruefully. "Come to think of it, I'll have one now. It'll make this easier."

The bartender laughed. "You're kidding right? Your

choices are beer, rum and coke, vodka and raspberry, or cask wine—both colors."

"Bundy and coke please. If I'm doing this, I'm doing it properly with Aussie rum." While she waited, Jen swiveled on her stool to check out the dance floor through the black gauzy peepholes. Both Beth and Ellie looked like they were having fun being whirled around by a couple of light-footed cowboys.

Light-handed, too, in Ellie's case. Her handsome dance partner's hand lay a little lower than was strictly platonic.

Gleefully, Jen rubbed her hooves together. "I do love it when a plan comes together." Much as she liked Rick, Ellie's childhood crush was overdue for a wake-up call. He was on the dance floor somewhere, it was only a matter of time before the cowpat hit the fan.

"That's an evil laugh." The barman plonked a rum and coke in front of her. "And kinda sexy. Are you cute under there by any chance?"

"Nope," Jen said cheerfully. "Hideous." She fumbled with the zipper on her udder pocket where she'd stashed her cash and cell phone, and dropped a ten dollar bill on the bar. "Since I have trouble handling coins, keep the change."

"Thanks!"

It took Jen a good minute to re-zip—why the hell didn't the costume have separate gloves instead of hooves stitched to the onesie? At least she was getting more adept manipulating the straw. She was sucking in a mouthful of rum and coke and grimacing at its sweetness when Beth glanced over her youthful dance partner's shoulder to check on her. Jen raised her plastic goblet in a toast and Beth grinned.

So what if this damn cow suit itched and was a practical nightmare if she could make Beth smile? Her friends had laughed until they'd cried when Jen sashayed out of the tent in costume and warned, "If Clarabelle's head is hanging outside the tent, you gals will just have to find somewhere else to sleep."

Bottom line? Her heartbreak was nothing to Beth's. Jen's humiliation had been witnessed by only a few dozen colleagues, not the whole world. And, unlike her friend who'd been crazy in love with her country rock star husband, Jen had held something back with Karl.

Her parents' divorce had taught her young that love was a risky business and everything that happened since—her failed relationship with Karl, Beth's cheating ex and Ellie's unrequited love for Rick—had only reinforced that conviction.

And yet…there was always this wistfulness when she saw older couples who'd lasted the distance. She watched one on the dance floor, early sixties maybe, ignoring the upbeat tempo and slow-dancing to their own tune. She did believe in true love…for those brave or lucky enough.

A man brushed past, walking away from her, his purposeful stride at such odds with the meandering party-goers that she was immediately reminded of the Terminator. He wore the formal suit as it should be worn, with an indifferent male grace and it didn't hurt that his shoulders filled the jacket nicely. His haircut was military short and Jen wasn't surprised when the security volunteer watching the dancers lost his bored expression and straightened, almost to attention.

Intrigued to see his face, she waited for the Terminator to turn. Someone bumped her from behind and her rum and coke splattered into her lap. "Careful!"

"Shit, sorry. It was an accident." Her young male assailant did a double take. "That's some outfit, mate."

"Don't you know cows are girls?" Grabbing a cocktail napkin from the bar, Jen dabbed at the sticky splotches on her hide.

"Course I know cows are girls," he said, reddening. He was young, maybe eighteen, rangy and long-boned and his too-big suit gave him the look of a scarecrow. "It's just usually the girls dress up for this. You know…to meet guys."

"Not me, I'm not interested," she said, wadding the tissue and dropping it into her now-empty goblet. "You hoping to meet someone?"

Clutching his schooner of beer tighter, he shuffled his feet. "I guess...I'm kinda learning the ropes."

"So you're a B&S virgin?"

His fiery color deepened. "W-what? Oh. Yeah. First time here. My brother bet me I wouldn't ask a girl to dance." Taking a slug of his beer, he glanced over to the gaggle of cute teens edging the dance floor with the awful fascination of a man faced with zombies.

Jen took pity on him. "Ask me, I'm a girl."

"Yeah." He looked her over doubtfully. "I'm not sure you'd count."

"C'mon," she encouraged. "I'll even take my head off." She did and smiled at him.

He blushed again.

"I'm twenty-eight," she encouraged, "that means I'm—"

"Old," he said with some relief. "Sorry, I meant that—"

Jen laughed. "What's your name?"

"Darryl."

"Come on, Darryl, let's at least get you closer to girls your own age."

Removing the schooner from his reluctant hands, she replaced Clarabelle's head—some clown would steal her if she left her here—and encouraged her shy swain to the dance floor, glancing around for her friends.

No sign of Beth, but Ellie and Rick were having an intense conversation in the far corner of the pavilion. Maybe the stubborn cowboy was finally coming to his senses.

Once Darryl's embarrassment subsided he proved to be a good dancer and Jen had fun mirroring his moves. His expression brightened as he recognized her skill and for a couple of songs they boogied with the best of them. The giggling teen girls on the sidelines noticed

Clarabelle and pointed and Darryl got a little carried away under the attention.

Grabbing her hand, he spun Jen into a twirl that sent her tail flying. The floor was slippery under hoof and she stumbled into another couple. Apologizing, she returned to her partner. "Steady, Darryl. As crazy as this sounds, I don't *want* to draw attention to myself."

"Ha," he said. "You're funny."

The song ended, giving Jen the chance to catch her breath. Dancing inside Clarabelle was like dancing wrapped in a duvet. "I'm not going to last much longer," she warned Darryl. "Too hot, too thirsty."

His face fell.

"How about we dance over to the girls, and I'll ask one of them to swap with me?" she suggested, as the next song started. "We'll keep it low key," she promised when his Adam's apple bobbed in a nervous swallow. "I'll tell them you need a real *moo*ver."

"That's a brilliant idea." Darryl swept Jen into a two-step and whirled a couple of tight circles toward the bystanders. Jen lost all sense of direction, and when he released her she careened into the girls, who shrieked theatrically as they all fell down.

So much for not drawing attention to herself.

She was on her knees, about to push to her feet when a firm hand grabbed the fabric between her shoulder blades and hauled her upright. "There are better ways to sweep a lady off her feet, mate."

The Terminator frowned at her. His eyes were Atlantic blue, in keeping with the implicit power of his warrior body and the vise-like grip on her clothing. For the first time, she noticed his security arm band. *Uh-oh.* "How about we step outside for some fresh air, and you can tell me how much you've had to drink."

His face was strong, his jaw and cheekbones as uncompromising as the rest of him. Jen had a nagging sense she should recognize him. "I've only had two sips of a rum and coke," she insisted. And the effects of this afternoon's wine had long since been sweated away. Jen checked her dance partner who was ignoring her in favor of picking up—literally—some fallen women. *Go Darryl.*

The tight grip on her cow suit released abruptly. "You're female."

Exasperation replaced embarrassment. "Hel-lo," Jen shook her udders at him, "I'm a *cow.*"

His eyes crinkled nicely when he smiled. "That explains it."

"Explains what?"

Placing a palm lightly on her back, he steered her clear of the dancers. "I saw you arrive and it bothered me that someone in that outfit could do so well with women."

The penny dropped. He was the same dark-haired hunk who'd frowned at her as she'd waltzed past between Ellie and Beth. They'd all noticed him—heck, even Jen had been tempted to swish her tail. Except he hadn't been looking at her. He'd been too busy checking out her girlfriends with the appreciative glint of a sex-starved male.

"I didn't recognize you with your mouth closed," she said.

He grinned, not denying it. "I've been in the desert for months."

"Next you'll be telling me about the horse with no name."

He chuckled. "Mine's Logan. And you are…?"

Oh, no, anonymity was all that protected the last shred of her dignity. She straightened Clarabelle's head. "If the horse won't tell you his name," she said reasonably, "why would you expect a cow to?"

His laugh was husky, as attractive as the rest of him. "Drink lots of water or you'll suffer heat exhaustion."

Come to think of it, she was feeling a little breathless. "Yes, sir, I'll go do that right now."

"Hey, mystery cow," Logan called after her. He held out her ear tag. "You lost this in the fall."

Bravado came easy when you couldn't make more of a fool of yourself. "Keep it as a souvenir, cutie."

His laugh followed her to the bar.

No way was Jen interested in men right now…and yet. She glanced over her shoulder. Logan was still grinning after her.

Jen drank water, which drove her to the Portaloo. Again. For Pete's sake, she was spending more time here, undressing and dressing, than she was at the ball. She paused outside, reluctant to don Clarabelle's head, but unwilling to be seen without it. Fumbling with the zipper on her udder pocket, she pulled her cell free and sent a text to her girls—a painstaking process given her padded thumb:

Going to the tent to change.

Beth replied immediately. *Need me to come, too?*

"Oh, no, you don't, missy," Jen said aloud and texted: *Remember the dare, dancing queen. Reclaim your power!*

Her cell beeped another incoming message, this one from Ellie.

Amazed you lasted this long. I always ditched the head within ten minutes when I wore Clarabelle.

"*Now* you tell me," Jen muttered. Laboriously, she texted a reply. *Best part is being able to return as a girl with no one the wiser.* She resisted the urge to scan the grounds for Logan, because that would be shallow. As she was reluctantly pulling on Clarabelle's head, another text from Beth beeped and she peered at it through the peepholes.

No sneaking off to bed if I can't.

The thought had crossed Jen's mind. She had the beginnings of a headache, which meant Logan was right; she was getting dehydrated. Once she reached the tent, she'd grab an aspirin and reassess the situation.

Collecting a pass for re-entry, Jen wandered across the square toward the gate, her progress slowed by constant requests for selfies. The drunker people got, the more they wanted to pose and joke with her, though if another person assumed she was a guy...

In the spirit of animal solidarity she paused to talk to a pink rabbit giving away free condoms. "These are country people," she confided, taking off Clarabelle's head to scratch an itch on her neck. "They should be able to recognize a cow from a bull."

"Tell me about it," the rabbit said, lining up the prophylactics in his wicker basket by color. "Everyone thinks I'm a girl just because I'm pink. It's bloody sexism."

"Why *are* you dressed as a bunny?" she asked curiously, replacing the cow's head.

"Boink like a rabbit. Breed like a rabbit...a carrot-stick kind of approach?" He shrugged narrow shoulders. "When you're promoting safe sex, you want to stand out and a costume guarantees attention. You've probably noticed."

"Oh, yeah... Oi!" Jen spun around as someone yanked her tail. "We don't know each other well enough for that."

"So you want a couple of these?" The rabbit showed her his basket. "We got ribbed, spotted, extra thin, latex free, fruity—"

"Thanks, but I'm on a break."

"You say that now. What about in a few hours when you've got your rosé-colored glasses on?"

Laughing, Jen declined, stepping back to allow a trio of young guys to stuff their pockets. Wishful thinking she suspected.

"I'll be here for the next few hours if you change your mind," the rabbit hollered after her, and she gave him the thumbs-up.

As she padded outside the entry gate toward the

campground, the music faded to a distant bass beat and she could hear herself breathing inside Clarabelle's furry skull. Every shadow seemed to hold a couple, passionately kissing. "Safe sex," she sang out to one pair who were all but horizontal. "Get condoms from the bunny." Somehow she'd begun enjoying herself, hidden behind Clarabelle's alter ego.

In the first picnic clearing, some happily inebriated cowboys had rigged up lighting and were taking turns dropping a lasso over a tent pole hammered into the ground. Jen paused to watch as one of them, beer bottle in one hand, flicked the rope over the peg with lazy precision.

As he wandered over to loosen it, he caught sight of Jen and grinned, pushing back his Akubra to reveal an untanned strip of white on his weathered forehead. "Separated from the herd?"

"Heading home from the range. Have a nice evening." With a friendly wave Jen resumed walking.

"I think it's a girl," someone commented.

"Nope, I'm a boy soprano from the Vienna Boys Choir," Jen flung over her shoulder and caught the Akubra-wearing cowboy whirling the lasso over his head. She stopped and wagged her mitten-hoof at him. "Don't even *think* about it."

One of his mates chuckled. "She's a feisty little heifer, Bill."

"She *is* feisty, Bill," Jen warned.

He doffed his hat, revealing a shaved head. "Go right ahead, ma'am."

She'd taken three steps when she heard the whistle of the rope. It flicked over Clarabelle's head and yanked tight pinning Jen's arms. "Hey!"

CHAPTER 4

BILL HOOTED. "IT'S WAY MORE fun with a moving target." He and his friends roared with laughter.

Wriggling her arms free, Jen tried to loosen the knot and failed. Damn these mittens. "Okay guys, you've had your fun. Now untie me."

"*Moove* over here then." Bill tugged and she jerked forward a couple of steps. The others howled.

She could choose anger or fear. Jen marched over, and the tail of the rope fell slackly to the ground. "You take this off me right now," she demanded.

The boys kept laughing.

"No need to get so *bull*igerant..." said Bill, sending them into more fits.

"She is *udderly* pissed with you, Bill."

The puns came thick and fast then, and it seemed the madder Jen got, the funnier these jokers found it.

Narrowing her eyes inside Clarabelle's head, Jen grabbed the loose rope and did a quick double twist around Bill's wrists. "How do *you* like being tied up?"

"Whoa, she's into bondage, Bill."

"Seriously," she said, "how old are you guys?" But the shift of innuendo toward the sexual frightened her. "Late twenties, early thirties and you're acting like kids." She didn't think they meant her any harm but her anger developed a desperate edge.

Bill wiped tears of laughter away from his eyes as he freed one hand. "Jus' a couple of photos please, honey. Lemme grab my cell."

But Jen had had enough. When he leaned in for the selfie, she head-butted him.

His hat toppled off. With a howl, Bill grabbed his face.

"Oh, *c'mon*," Jen threw up her mittens in disgust. "My head's padded."

Clutching his left eye, Bill glared reproachfully from his right, which was tearing up. "You gored me with your horn."

"Jeez, we were just having a little fun." With a hurt look, one of his mates untied the rope around her middle. "There wasn't any harm in it."

Jen put her hooves on her hips. "I don't know you," she said. "And it stopped being funny for me when I said 'let me go' and you didn't. Another woman might find that scary and threatening and you guys are old enough to *know* that." Someone went to speak and she turned on him. "And do *not* use alcohol as an excuse."

As she glared around the circle, a few of them mumbled apologies.

"Is my eye okay?" The rope still looped around his wrist, Bill took his hand away. It was red and puffy and weeping and his mates winced. Two took a step back.

"Oh, for heaven's sake," Jen said, exasperated. "*I'll* take you to the first aid tent." Grabbing his arm she turned and walked straight into Logan. He looked at Bill clutching his face, the rope around his wrist, and then at Jen. "Let me guess," he said. "It wasn't your fault."

"It wasn't," Bill mumbled. "We kinda—"

"All sorted now," Jen said. "Or will be once Bill gets to first aid."

Logan looked at the coil of rope on the ground. "You sure?" There was a wealth of help in his quiet inquiry, mixed with a menace that made Jen shiver, though it wasn't directed at her. The other guys shuffled and looked at their feet.

"I'm sure."

Logan turned to the closest cowboy. "You. Take him to the med tent."

"Sure." The guy all but bowed in his eagerness to placate.

"I'll come!"

"Me, too." A stampede of volunteers joined him, two pausing to mumble apologies to Jen.

She and Logan were left alone.

"I'm on my way to the tent to change," she said, to circumvent a lecture.

"A woman should be able to dress how she wants and remain unmolested," he commented, passing a water bottle from hand to hand. "But wandering past some wranglers in a cow costume is really pushing it."

"Which is why I let them off the hook."

He smiled. The Terminator had a killer smile. "Getting dizzy under all that wadding yet?"

"A little," she admitted.

"Sit down a minute." He cleared a wooden trestle seat of empty beer cans and gave her the water bottle. "I was looking for you to give you this."

She was touched. "Thank you, I am thirsty." She wrestled with the cap and he took it from her.

"Let me."

Shyly, Jen removed Clarabelle's head. "So you patrol outside, too?"

"It's where the wild things are." He handed her the opened bottle.

While she hadn't thought he'd gasp and say, "My God you're beautiful," Jen was a little piqued when Logan's laughter lines deepened. Surreptitiously, she checked out her appearance in the side mirror of an adjacent ute. Red-faced, hair plastered to her skull. An internal seam had pressed a Frankenstein scar across her forehead.

How lucky that she wasn't interested in men anytime soon.

"This may come as a surprise to you," she said, pausing with the bottle to her lips. "But in my real life I'm considered dignified and sensible."

"Yeah? I don't see you as the quiet type myself."

Ignoring the crack, she drank thirstily, moaning aloud with the pleasure of it. "Thank you, this is so good."

Logan took a moment to answer. "You're welcome." His walkie-talkie crackled and he wandered out of earshot to accept the call. Something in the way he moved stirred an emotion. If Jen wasn't on a man-ban, she'd have called it lust. She forced her gaze to her lap and met Clarabelle's accusatory stare. "Hey, I can still look," she muttered.

"Look at what?"

Jen started and Clarabelle's head rolled off her lap. "The stars," she said, picking up Clarabelle and brushing the dust off her eyelashes. "They're beautiful tonight." Great, now he'd caught her talking to the cow.

He looked up. Even the long column of his throat was sexy. "Very pretty. Listen, there's trouble brewing around the bar, otherwise I'd walk you to your tent."

"I'm fine," she waved airily. "You go. Save other species." She proffered her mitten-hoof. "It's Jen. My name."

They shook solemnly, then Logan reached out and brushed a damp strand of hair from her cheek. His fingers were rough, calloused and thrilling against her skin. *Heat exhaustion,* she thought. *Has to be.*

"Take care, Jen."

"See you around, Logan."

She watched him walk away, quietly appalled at herself. It took her at least a year to get over a guy; she couldn't possibly be so attracted to someone a mere month after Karl. Could she?

She shook off the thought then faced the camping ground and tried to get her bearings.

It had filled to overflowing since they'd pitched their tent, changing the entire configuration. Had there been an identifying landmark? Yes, a line of gum trees.

The light cast by the cowboys' floodlights faded into blackness past the picnic area. All she could see was the odd lantern illuminating a tent and the bounce of flashlights as other party-goers picked their way through the campground.

Damn. Ellie had their small flashlight in her clutch.

Jen fumbled with the zip on her udder to retrieve her cell. Maybe its thin beam would be good enough. These stupid mittens were like wearing oven gloves. The zip caught in the faux fur and stuck. No amount of yanking, tugging and cursing made a difference. Sucking up her frustration, Jen tucked Clarabelle's head under one arm and trudged back toward the pavilion.

At the entry gate, a thin security guard with a goatee swaggered into her path, a walkie-talkie hanging from his belt like a gun holster. In addition to the fluorescent arm band and tag proclaiming him security, he wore a black cap with *Make My Day* embroidered across it. "No re-admittance after nine."

"Where does it say that?"

He pointed to the sign attached to the gate. STRICTLY, NO RE-ENTRY PERMITTED AFTER NINE!

Jen pleaded, she argued, she even tried flirting. Like that would work. The security guard remained adamant. Hitching his pants, he hooked a thumb in his belt. "If I make an exception for you, little lady, I'd have to do it for everyone."

Little lady? Even with a goatee, the guy looked only nineteen. But his officiousness prompted an idea. "I'm actually part of the security detail. Congratulations—" Jen turned over his name tag, "—Wayne. You've passed the test with flying colors."

Wayne snorted. "Yeah right. Where's *your* badge, then?"

"Dude." Jen indicated her outfit. "Clearly, I'm undercover."

"Nice try, beef cheeks, but there are no flies on this volunteer."

Reluctantly, Jen played her trump card. "Call Logan." *Please don't ask for his last name.* "He'll vouch for me."

Wayne unhooked his thumb from his belt. "You know Lily's brother?"

"Would I be throwing his name around so freely if I didn't?"

"You serve together?"

Jen racked her brains. *Serve drinks? Serve food? Serves me right?* "Me and Logan go back a long way," she said vaguely. Inside her hoof-mitten, Jen crossed fingers. The past hour had *felt* like weeks, so surely that counted for something.

Wayne unhitched his walkie-talkie. "Stay where I can keep an eye on you," he warned and Jen nodded. This guy watched way too many crime shows.

"Logan, this is going to sound really crazy, but I've got a cow here saying she's testing security measures and that you'd vouch for her." Small, suspicious eyes met Jen's; she affected nonchalance. "Uh-huh." Wayne's attention returned to the conversation. "Okay then."

Re-holstering the walkie-talkie, he folded his arms. "He's coming."

"Great." Jen adjusted her udders and thought weakly, great.

Resting a scrawny arm on the gate post, Wayne leaned forward. "So," he said confidentially, "How was it in Iraq?"

"Dusty?"

"Fine, take the piss," he grumbled and ignored her in favor of adjusting his walkie-talkie settings.

Ten minutes later, Logan strolled over. Jen couldn't quite meet his gaze, but oh, boy, she felt it. He spoke to the security guard. "Nice job, mate."

Wayne hooked two thumbs in his belt. "I don't mind admitting, Logan, she nearly got past me."

What?

"Well, she's highly trained."

Jen bit her lip to match Logan's implacable expression.

"And those big brown eyes are a killer," he added dryly.

A gurgle of laughter escaped, which Jen turned into a cough.

"Fur ball?" Logan inquired silkily. Catching her elbow, he congratulated Wayne again—"Keep up the good work, mate"—and steered her away.

The smile curving his lips did funny things to her insides. "What happened this time?" he asked, when they were out of earshot.

"I couldn't find the tent without a flashlight, then the zipper stuck on this suit so I couldn't phone my friends." She fumbled with the zip again. "I don't suppose you carry scissors? I'd kill to get my hands free."

Without a word, he pulled out a Swiss army knife and flicked it open. The steel gleamed like his eyes. "Yes?"

"Yes." Dumping Clarabelle's head on the ground, Jen stuck out her hands. "I'll buy Ellie new gloves."

Efficiently, he sliced through the seams around her wrists and freed her hands. Jen tugged at the zipper. "Still jammed."

"Wait here." Logan disappeared into a nearby toilet block and reappeared with a dab of liquid soap in his palm, which he ran over the zip.

"Always prepared?"

"Something like that." He started working the zipper. If his hair was longer it would have a wave in it. Jen recalled Wayne's comment. "You're a soldier."

"Not anymore."

His shampoo had base notes of pine—surreptitiously she breathed deeper. Or it could be his aftershave. Or him.

She felt a sudden helplessness and didn't like it. "Let me hold the fabric away as you pull the zip," she insisted and Logan took a half-step back to make space and Jen could breathe again. "I've never been involved in screwball escapades before," she told him as they worked in tandem. *At least, not since boarding school.*

He didn't lift his head. "I've never worked security where a cow keeps getting into trouble either."

Hearing the lilt of laughter in his voice, Jen relaxed. "So we're both treading new ground tonight."

Logan looked up, his dark blue irises fathomless. "I think maybe we are," he said slowly.

She'd snorkeled the Great Barrier Reef, and the sensation she had now was like looking over the ledge of friendly coral to where the reef fell away—the same lurch of her stomach, the same awe spiked with disquiet.

Involuntarily, her fingers tightened. The zipper pulled free of the fabric and opened, spilling the contents—her cell and some notes and coins.

Logan helped her pick everything up. "I'm adding my number," he said, tapping it into her cell before returning it. "In case you find yourself in more trouble."

"Give me your cell," she ordered, piqued at his assumption. She brought up his phone contacts. "Here's mine in case you want to go *looking* for trouble."

"Are you *flirting* with me?" Amusement deepened the blue of his eyes and Jen allowed herself a brief immersion.

"Sure," she said. "Why not?"

He grinned. "I can't leave my post."

Of course she knew that. No way would she be this reckless otherwise. Jen twirled Clarabelle's tail in his direction. "But you're tempted, am I right?"

His laugh was a shout of pure joy. Chuckling, she returned to the pavilion in search of her friends and a decent flashlight. No sign of Beth, and Ellie sat at one of the tables, locking lips with Rick's friend Jack. Jen gave a silent whistle. So Rick had ceded the game. The closet romantic in Jen was sad about that, but at least Ellie wasn't wasting her twenties pining anymore.

Clearly, now wasn't the best time to interrupt but— Jen wiggled her fingers, enjoying the freedom of movement—she had hands now, dexterity, heck, she could wait. She threaded through the crowded bar and stood patiently in the queue.

As she ordered an orange juice, the bartender said, "Hey, you are cute."

"Thank you."

"Ladies and gentlemen," the MC bellowed from the stage. "We have got a *massive* surprise for you tonight."

The bartender gave Jen her change. "You're gonna want to hear this," he said, his excitement palpable.

"As some of you may know," said the MC, "we had Leonie Kingston booked, but she came down with the flu this week and had to pull out."

The crowd booed. "Because it's all about us," Jen murmured to the bartender.

"Ironic too," he said with an approving nod. "But listen…"

"…We were able to line up a new act to step in at the last minute. I think you're going to be pretty happy, people," the MC continued. "Put your hands together for our own local boys made good, Jonah Masters and the Rowdy Boys!"

Jen led the roar of approval. The Rowdy Boys were one of her favorite country rock bands. The night was definitely looking up.

Clarabelle's head under her arm, she craned her neck for a better view.

A tipsy young woman edged beside her at the bar. "Seriously cool outfit," she shouted over the applause. "Want to swap?"

"No offense, but I'm over the jokes." Jen sidestepped to join the surge toward the stage.

"I'm serious." The brunette fell into step beside her.

"I had way more fun last year in costume than tarted up in a bridesmaid dress I hated first time round."

As the band took their positions, Jen stopped and stared at her. Slightly more buxom than Jen, but only an inch or two taller. Eighteen, nineteen with a round, friendly face. Her gown was pretty, but in a color that didn't suit her—a bronze satin that brought out her freckles. Something about her reminded Jen of Ellie, the confidence maybe, or the mischief in her eyes.

"You'll be teased," she warned.

The younger woman shrugged. "I'm a country girl, I can handle myself," she said. "Besides, I'm here with my posse." She indicated a raucous group by the door, sniggering among themselves, a couple of solid boys among them.

As Jen considered the idea, the Rowdy Boys struck up their first number, adding to the temptation. She could stay and enjoy the band's whole set, dance even. *Maybe exchange more banter with the sexy security guard as a woman.* "I'd need the cow costume returned," she hollered over the music. "I borrowed it from a friend."

"Sure," the younger woman shouted. "We can rendezvous in the morning and swap back. She stuck out a hand, calloused and manicured. "I'm Kylie."

"Jen." They shook. "Okay, let's do this," Jen handed over Clarabelle's head. With a whoop, Kylie turned to give her friends a big thumbs-up and teetered dangerously. Jen grabbed her elbow to stop her falling. Either Kylie wasn't used to wearing stilettos or she was drunker than she looked.

Would she remember to return Clarabelle tomorrow? Jen begged some paper and a pen off the bartender and hastily wrote her details.

Accompanied by one of Kylie's girlfriends—a giggling blonde—they went outside to adjacent Portaloos to change. Inside her stall, Jen stripped to her underwear and opened the door a crack. "You ready, Kylie?"

Her friend stepped forward holding out Kylie's shoes and stole. "Nearly, she's having a bit of trouble with the zip."

Passing over the onesie, Jen reached for the other items at the same time. As her fingertips brushed the stole, the blonde jerked it away. "Sucker!"

Chortling, Kylie reappeared fully dressed. As Jen watched, shocked, the two women did an unsteady runner with Clarabelle. "Sorry," Kylie yelled over her shoulder, "but a dare's a dare and we need the pay-out for more beer."

Jen was so wild she'd shoved the door open to give chase before she remembered her underwear was semi-transparent. "I hope you get foot-rot, pinkeye *and* parasites," she yelled. Catching some passers-by gawking, she slammed the door shut again, fuming. She would call in reinforcements, organize her own posse. Those kids would be so sorry when Logan caught... Her fingers hovered over her midriff where her udder pocket should be. Jen groaned.

The udder pocket that held her cell and money.

CHAPTER 5

"**I WANT TO TAKE A** cow for a drink." Logan hauled his sister outside, interrupting her ogle of the band's lead singer. "I don't care if you have to deputize a two-year-old, find someone else to relieve me."

Lily stared at him. "Are you drunk?"

"No," he said wryly, "but I might be smitten."

Briefly, he filled her in on Jen. "It sounds crazy but if I don't follow up on this, I'll regret it."

"Wow, you don't do impulsive, she must be seriously hot."

Logan grinned, recalling Jen's face when she'd pulled off the cow's head. "She *was* hot," he agreed. Cleaned up, she'd probably be a looker, but he wanted to spend time with her because she'd given him the most entertainment he'd had in months. "But it's her personality I'm attracted to."

His sister laid her hand on his brow. "Not feverish," she marveled, and he shook her off.

"Stop making me out to be shallow," he said. "I haven't had time for long-term relationships."

"You want the cow to be your girlfriend?"

Folding his arms, Logan gave her the stare.

He'd liked the cow the moment she sassed him on the dance floor and with every encounter since his enjoyment of Jen had grown. He had no idea what she'd do or say next, only that it would be entertaining.

His impulse to track her down and give her water had been an altruistic one—dehydration was a real danger in that suit—but the small moan she'd given as she'd taken her first gulp had caught him by surprise. There had been something intriguingly sensual in her pleasure.

When she'd finally introduced herself and they'd shaken hands, Logan hadn't been able to resist the impulse to brush a loose tendril from her face. Her skin had been like touching silk.

Summoned by Jen to rescue her from Wayne's over-zealous application of the rules, Logan had relished teasing her into 'breaking cover.' But when he'd told Wayne "those big brown eyes are killer" he'd been perfectly serious.

Lily succumbed to the stare. "Fine," his sister stopped teasing him. "It'll be tough, but I'll see what I can do." Like she was the one doing him the massive favor here.

"I have every faith in your ability to press-gang volunteers," he retorted and she pretended not to hear.

Logan walked outside for privacy and phoned Jen's cell.

"Yeahwhatchawant?" A male voice.

"Is this Jen's number?" It occurred to Logan that he didn't know her last name.

A moment's hesitation. "Nah," the guy said hastily, "never heard of her." He ended the call.

Logan returned to Lily. "Forget about finding a replacement, she gave me a fake number." *And I'm a dumbass.* As soon as Jen had said, "We're both treading new ground tonight," the words resonated. He'd have sworn she felt the same mysterious connection. *I've definitely been in the desert too long.*

"No," Lily said. "I've been taking you for granted and you deserve a break. Tracy's dad will take over the rest of your shift if you do his tomorrow morning. Be at the security tent by seven-thirty."

"The rest of my shift?" Logan repeated. "You told me two hours."

"It will *definitely* be no more than two tomorrow." Lily promised earnestly. "Helping stragglers decamp, making sure no idiot does circle work or car surfs…everything *you* used to do."

"Quit pretending to be the grownup here."

"Hey, I'm not the one attracted to a cow's personality." Lily pushed him toward the pavilion. "Go. Find a real woman to dance to The Rowdy Boys with. Have a drink."

"Sounds good," he said. The bar at least. At the security tent he surrendered his armband and walkie-talkie to Wayne. Lily had really scraped the bottom of the volunteer barrel with the goateed gamer who seemed to be channeling *Call of Duty*, even asking Logan for a debrief.

He obliged, throwing in military terms and the twenty-four hour clock. Someone might as well have a good night. Logan was strolling to the pavilion—and the bar—when he spotted Clarabelle walking toward him. For a moment, he was pissed—why did Jen plug her number into his cell if she was going to use a fake one?—then he shrugged it off. Jen didn't owe him anything. "Hey, there." He smiled as they drew closer. "How's your night going?"

She raised a thumb and kept on walking. Okay, that was weird. Logan turned to stare after her.

Something was different. It took him another second to work it out, then his eyes narrowed. The cow no longer walked like a woman. In a few quick steps, he caught up and grabbed Clarabelle's shoulder. "Who the hell are you, and where is Jen?"

The guy blustered. "Mate, Jen and me, we swapped clothes. She's around somewhere."

"Yeah? So why were you answering her cell? Don't deny it, I recognize your voice."

With the stare, it took five minutes to get the truth. He'd dared a friend thirty bucks she couldn't get him the cow costume. Until Logan's call they hadn't realized she'd also stolen Jen's money and phone. They'd gotten worried about being tracked through the cell's GPS and ditched the cell in a tub of melting ice.

Logan delivered him to the security tent—Wayne would put the fear of God into him until Tim the security chief arrived to deal with him and his friends—and strode swiftly along the line of Portaloos, softly calling Jen's name.

Given her resourcefulness, she'd probably enlisted the help of a passer-by and borrowed some clothes by now. He didn't need to worry so-

"I'm here."

Logan was suddenly very glad he'd handed the young fool over for processing, minus Jen's cash. The tell-tale quiver in her voice tempted him to violence. He paused in front of the last door. "You'll be pleased to hear that Clarabelle's safe," he said, "if slightly beer-sodden." Alcohol also explained why the guy never questioned the unwisdom of wearing a stolen cow suit.

"Did you bring her? I really need clothes."

Now that was something he should have thought of. "Hang on." Logan stripped off his jacket, then his shirt before tapping on the door. "Here."

A slender arm reached out and took his shirt.

Shrugging his jacket over his bare torso, he said quietly, "The clowns who took Clarabelle threw your cell away in a panic, but I expect they'll be very keen to replace it to avoid the police getting involved. Unless you want to press charges?"

"No." Jen opened the door and stepped out, her feet bare. The tail of his white dress shirt covered her smooth legs to mid-thigh. Though she'd splashed her face with water, her reddened eyes told their own story. She managed a wobbly smile. "We've got to stop meeting like this."

Her bravado kicked up his protective instincts like nothing else. There was something so cute and feisty and classy about this woman. She was in a ridiculous situation, and still punching through it. Instinctively, he drew her into a hug. "Don't let those young idiots ruin your evening."

She stiffened in his arms. "We don't know each other," she said in a surprised voice.

"You're right," Logan said. The oldest in a large family, he was used to casual affection; clearly Jen wasn't. Resisting the urge to kiss the top of her head, he released her. "I'm sorry."

A blush in her cheeks, she patted his arm awkwardly. "Seems like every time I've got into trouble tonight you manage to track me down and save me." She forced a laugh. "You're like Daniel Day Lewis in *The Last of the Mohicans* where he promises to find Madeleine Stowe." Another wobbly smile. "I'm the one who should be apologizing for being so much trouble."

She was stealing his heart, piece by piece, and there was nothing he could do.

"Much as I'd like to be the hero, you've handled every other situation yourself." Digging in his pants pocket, he returned her money.

Her smile steadied as she took them. "You think?"

"Oh sure, I've just been the sidekick." Someone should be giving this woman a hug if he couldn't—she was more shaken than she was letting on. "Want to call your friends on my cell?"

She shook her head. "No need to spoil their evening, especially since I'm fine." She added briskly, "I'm going to call it a night, go crawl into my sleeping bag."

Logan wondered how often she allowed herself to show weakness. It was something he struggled with himself. "How are you going to find your tent?"

"Good point." Thinking, she raked a hand through her dark hair. It had fluffed into a soft tousled fall since he'd last seen her. "Can you lend me a flashlight?"

"I'll do better than that. I'll walk you."

"Aren't you working?"

"I'm off." What the hell, no one died of humiliation. "Actually, I was intending to ask you for a drink."

"Really?" Momentarily, delight warmed her dark eyes, warmed *him*. Then Jen's gaze slid away as though her recent embarrassment got the better of her. She grimaced. "As you can see, I'm not dressed for it."

"I can fix that." Digging in his jacket pocket, Logan found his discarded bow tie. He fastened the two top buttons on her shirt and added the tie solemnly while Jen tried not to smile. "Now you meet the dress code," he said.

"I don't know." She glanced at her bare legs, her bare feet. "I'm kinda done being laughed at," she admitted.

"I understand." He tried to keep the disappointment from his voice.

"Unless…" She looked up. "You have a comb?"

"No." Logan ran a hand over his short hair. "But I know where to get one."

He phoned his sister and begged a comb, which she delivered personally, probably so she could take a look at Jen. "Here," Lily said to her. "Borrow my lipstick and blush too."

While Jen was applying make-up, Logan took Lily aside. "If you love me, give me your wrap and shoes."

She heaved a long-suffering sigh and murmured he owed her big time, before handing over the goods.

Jen blinked when he presented them. "I feel like Cowderella and you're my fairy godfather."

"Lose the fairy part, it's cramping my style."

She slanted him a sideways look, partly intrigued, partly wary, as she stepped into Lily's sparkling shoes. God bless his impractical sister; they were stilettos and lengthened Jen's legs to fantasy proportions. "Are you flirting with me?"

"Sure," Logan echoed her earlier challenge. "Why not?"

One hand went automatically to her hair. Why did women always do that? As though neat and tidy was what guys noticed. Catching her fingers, Logan tucked her arm firmly through his. "Let's go for that drink," he said, "and you can tell me his name."

Jen looked at him sharply. "Whose name?"

"The guy you're punishing by wearing the cow suit."

"You're wrong," Jen said when they'd settled at the bar with a drink.

Sadly, the band had finished their set, but Logan had rustled up decent red wine, "My sister has a secret stash." He drank beer, saying the coldness was still a novelty.

"I wore the cow suit on a dare. It's a thing my friends and I have from our old boarding school days." She filled him in on details—including leaving for New Zealand—keeping her tone upbeat and positive.

"Yes, it *is* true that we're all recently disappointed in love. The three dares are partly a big 'screw you' to the guys but they're also a way of reminding ourselves that we're in charge of our destinies." Jen recalled that Logan had witnessed every sorry incident of her night and ruefully tugged down the tail of his shirt. "That was the *plan* anyway."

Fingers crossed her besties were having better luck.

"The night's young," he said. "And you definitely have powers, if you can charm me into going AWOL." He told her about Lily press-ganging him into service, making her laugh.

The moment he'd brushed by, Jen had found him attractive—in a self-contained, controlled-power kind of way. Lounging in a chair, minus a shirt under his formal jacket, telling stories against himself, he was dangerously, devastatingly sexy. His torso alone was the stuff of female fantasy, as cut as the carved breastplate of ancient warriors.

Even inoculated to the charms of the male sex by her recent disillusionment, Jen enjoyed the view. And it didn't hurt her bruised ego to watch women doing a double take as they walked by, then share a grin of mutual female appreciation. Truly the male form could be a wondrous thing.

She'd never met a guy so...*male* and something in his eyes, an appreciation, a focus, made her feel fluttery in a way she'd never experienced. Despite her glossy grooming regime, Jen didn't consider herself a girly-girl but around Logan she felt all woman. And more oddly, she felt protected.

Logan refilled her wine glass. "I gather the breakup was recent."

"A month ago." So how could she be experienced such an intense attraction to another man so soon after Karl?

He replaced the bottle on the table. "And you're not over him?"

"Actually, Karl did a damn fine job of trampling any residual tender feelings," she replied. Maybe that was it, Karl had created a vacuum and Logan, with his larger-than-life presence, was filling it. "We worked together, and when he ditched me for his ex-wife, he suggested I quit my job so he wouldn't feel uncomfortable."

Logan raised an eyebrow. "And you did? That doesn't fit with the Clarabelle I've come to know."

Oh, she *liked* the way he saw her. "I did it for his kids. The sexual politics of adults isn't something you should have to deal with when you're still learning to read." Jen hesitated. This was stuff she didn't usually talk about but what the hell, they were never going to see each other again. And she instinctively trusted Logan's discretion. "My parents divorced over Dad's infidelity when I was young and it was...messy for all of us."

Despite the scars left on her psyche she wasn't

willing to attribute blame. They'd all suffered. "Being the other woman, even inadvertently, hits a nerve. Takes me someplace I swore I'd never go." *Okay, Jen, strike a positive note.* "But Karl did teach me one valuable lesson."

"What's that?"

"I can't stand the heat, so I'm staying out of the kitchen." Jen checked her wine-glass. Half-full, so this intimacy wasn't due to alcohol. It was him. She gave him a rueful smile. "Stop being such a good listener." God, those eyes, she could drown in them, warm, serious, understanding.

Logan returned her smile. "Maybe you were just cooking with the wrong guy," he said.

"But I chose him so *carefully*," she protested, straightening on the bar stool. The injustice still rankled. "He'd been divorced two years. Done the rebound flings." She ticked off the list on her fingers. "Never talked about his ex. We were friends first—"

"Tell me something," Logan said, cutting her off mid-outrage. "Were you attracted to this guy or did he just fit the algorithms?"

Jen laughed, a little sheepishly. "It wasn't *completely* clinical, Karl did have nice arms." *Not as nice as yours.* She tore her gaze away. "This 'safety first' mentality probably sounds crazy to you, right?"

"Why?"

"You're in the military. That implies a willingness to take risks."

"As of last month I became a civilian again." He toasted her with his beer. "But soldiers are the ultimate control freaks. Every decision you make in the field is potentially life or death so you train obsessively for every possible contingency. You get very good at situational awareness."

"For example?"

Logan could have said she used a rosemary shampoo and smelled faintly of disinfectant from hiding out in the

Portaloo. He could have mentioned the suggestion of a black lacy bra under the fine fabric of his dress shirt. "I know where all the exits are."

"Phh," she waved a dismissive hand. "Don't all guys know that?"

He laughed, enjoying her. It was hot in the pavilion and she'd tied Lily's shiny wrap around her waist, emphasizing her slim curves. Something about his shirt on her body made him feel protective, proprietary. Her hair fell like silk over the stiff white collar in glossy spills of molten caramel.

Even in a cow costume, she'd been graceful. In his shirt she was strikingly feminine, her long, shapely legs twined around the bar stool. Thanks to some indecisive douchebag, she was heartsore and wary. Not to mention leaving for New Zealand within twenty-four hours.

"I'm sorry you've had such a hard time," he said. *Damn sorry.*

"It's no big deal really, other people have it worse." She uncrossed her legs, re-crossed them. "I mean, we went out only a year and it's not like Karl had made me any promises or we were engaged or—"

"Stop letting the son-of-a-bitch off the hook," Logan said, angry on her behalf. "If he lived nearby, we could go plant the cow's head in his bed."

Jen laughed. "I think you're confusing your godfathers."

"I'm reinterpreting my role." *Time to lay his cards on the table.* "Paternal's not working for me."

Pink tinted her cheeks. "I think poor Clarabelle has suffered enough," she said lightly. For a moment she toyed with the stem of her plastic goblet, then looked up, her smile bright and impersonal. "So what about you? Married, engaged, going steady…pining for someone?"

He was starting to. "I wouldn't have asked you for a drink if I was."

"Sorry." Her mouth twisted. "I've become a little cynical."

And who could blame her? "My job meant being deployed for up to six months a year, so temporary's been the default on romance. Until now." Deliberately, Logan added the qualifier. Putting it out there. *Are you feeling this too?*

"People talk about meeting the right person," Jen said, "but timing is just as important."

They looked at each other and a wealth of understanding passed between them. Yeah, she felt this too. No, she wasn't doing anything about it because she was too gun-shy to risk another failure.

"I am very good at temporary," Logan said easily, ignoring his disappointment. She needed to understand he wasn't like Karl, all about his own interests. "Know what you need, Cowderella? A rebound guy." If nothing else, he could help restore her faith in men. Show her a fun time.

"What services does a rebound guy offer exactly?" she said cautiously.

"A little dancing, some major flirting, nothing that would tripwire the charges around your comfort zone."

Jen's chuckle was a warm, rich sound. "Hmm, if it's not risky, then why am I nervous?"

Logan believed in open communication. "Because at some point I'll probably try and kiss you."

Her eyes widened. "Unless," she said. "I kiss you first."

The Terminator's dark blue gaze kindled. "Unless you kiss me first," he agreed cordially.

"I'm so sorry," Jen blurted, "I shouldn't have said that." She still couldn't believe she had. "I'm not interested in a hookup and I'd hate to mislead you, especially when you've been so kind."

Logan leaned forward. Her heart kicked against her

ribs in a horrible jumble of panic and curiosity, but he bypassed her lips to murmur in her ear. "Then let's agree that only you initiate a kiss." He sat back, spread his hands. "Or not. I have no expectations, Jen."

"You're too easy to joke with," she accused, still flustered. "Normally the only time I let my hair down is with my girlfriends."

"Just to be clear," Logan said solemnly. "I am *not* one of your girlfriends. I may have no expectations, but my intentions are strictly dishonorable. I won't use subterfuge or false promises to sweet-talk my way into your sleeping bag, but I *will* take advantage if you give me any encouragement. I'm telling you this because I'm a straightforward guy. What you see is what you get."

There was a lot to get. Riches. Was she really going to pass up a fun few hours with him? "You have good wrapping," she said meekly and he laughed.

"And I'm a gift that keeps on giving."

"Wow, that cheesy line get you anywhere with women you're actually trying to impress?"

"I'm out of practice. Tonight will get me up to speed for real dating."

"Well, if I'm doing *you* a service as well," she said. Clearly, he understood the rules, and she desperately needed fun. "Okay, rebound guy, you're on. Let's hit the dance floor." The original band had retaken the stage and needed some encouragement.

"Just to tell you," he said, rising. "I have many, *many* mad skills. Dancing is not one of them."

Two dances later, Jen decided Logan's wooden moves had more to do with self-consciousness than a lack of co-ordination. It was pointless telling him that no one was looking. Every female within range was enjoying the view of his bare chest under the tuxedo jacket.

Jen caught his hands, encouraging him to focus on her and led him into a couple of simple moves, then raised his left arm to twirl under it. His limbs loosened as he concentrated on keeping up with her. Definitely, those hips had potential, she thought wickedly. He proved a fast learner. By the last chorus they had a simple routine going and as the song ended, he double-twirled her into his arms with a stylish flourish.

Logan grinned at her, a lazy grin that slid through her libido like a hot knife through butter. Resisting the urge to melt against him, Jen stepped back and applauded. "Keep this up and you'll be adding dancing to your mad skills."

"I have a good teacher...You want to stay for another?"

But she'd recognized the opening bars. The next tune was a slow, sexy ballad and her self-control needed reinforcing. "I'm thirsty. Let's take a break."

Logan placed a palm on the small of her back, inviting her to precede him. The light touch burned like a brand. *Control,* Jen reminded herself. *It's what you're good at.*

CHAPTER 6

"I'M TRYING TO MAKE OUT your accent," Logan said when they'd retaken their seats. "You have Australian intonations but you said earlier you were going home to New Zealand."

"Dad's a Kiwi and Mum's an Aussie." Jen filled two water glasses from the jug he'd bought over. "I went to her old boarding school here when I was twelve, and I've mostly lived here ever since."

"Twelve?" he said. "No offense, but what the hell were your parents thinking?"

"They weren't," she said. "They were in the middle of that messy divorce I mentioned. But thanks to boarding school I gained two sisters, the friends I'm camping with. And my parents are now happily married to other people. We're close again."

"Really?" Logan said. "I figured you wouldn't be."

"They did what they thought was best at the time," she said. "It was the *wrong* thing," she added ruefully, "but their hearts were in the right place." She'd had to grow up and take a few wrong turns of her own before she appreciated the distinction. Jen leaned forward. "So tell me about your family. I've met Lily. Any other siblings?"

"I'm the oldest of four, two boys, two girls," Logan

said. "Lily's the youngest." He talked about them for a few minutes while Jen listened, fascinated by childhood tales of pranks and counter-pranks, often instigated or adjudicated by Logan as the playfully affectionate big brother. "My parents own a cattle station in Queensland and have been together since they were eighteen. They met at one of these events."

"Really?" she said, delighted. "How romantic."

"I thought you were a cynic."

"Only for myself. So, what did you do for school?"

"Correspondence. I joined the Australian Army when I was eighteen, and they trained me as a mechanical engineer. When I was twenty-three I applied for the Special Air Service Regiment, the SAS."

"Special Services," Jen said. That explained a lot. The self-mastery he emanated, the quiet competence. He was someone people instinctively looked to for leadership—his sister, that crazy volunteer, Wayne. "You said you're a civilian now? What prompted you to leave?"

A shadow crossed his face.

"Don't tell me if you don't want to," she said immediately. "I completely understand the need for privacy." Too many people had asked her how she was feeling lately, meaning well, but raising the lid on painful emotions.

"A good friend—a fellow team member—died eighteen months ago in an ambush."

"I'm sorry," she said softly.

"The short version is, I could feel myself becoming embittered...desensitized." Logan hesitated. "This might sound a little crazy but I didn't want to lose touch with the values I'd sworn to defend." He gave her a tight smile. "Stop being such a good listener."

"It's freeing talking to a person you'll never see again...strangers in the night syndrome."

"I've done plenty of strangers in the night," Logan said dryly, "and this is very different."

She couldn't deny it, so Jen steered the conversation into safer channels. "So what have you been doing since you left?"

The tension in his expression eased. "Playing," he admitted. "This is the first time in my life I've had no responsibilities so I'm taking a few months to travel while I consider my career options. I could work as an engineer. Or I could set up a small business based on my SAS expertise—security, gun shop, parachute-packers."

He grinned. "Dad's also offering the carrot of a shareholding to return to the family station, but I'm not sure I'm ready to settle in one place yet. The idea of working in adventure tourism also appeals, I have tracking and bush craft expertise."

"*Lots* of mad skills," Jen said, impressed.

Logan shrugged. "Practical ones, anyway."

She found herself looking at his hands, blunt and square, strong. There were scars on his thumb, on impulse she traced them. "Where did these come from?"

"I'd love to say battle scars but I drove a tricycle through the sliding door when I was three."

Her fingers still touching his skin, Jen looked up with a grin. Once she'd watched a bush fire roar across a valley, dangerously beautiful. The wind changed and even miles away, she felt the wall of fierce heat that sucked all the oxygen out of her lungs. Looking into Logan's eyes was like that—intense, immediate and breathtaking.

His hand closed over hers, his thumb gently circled the fleshy part of her palm. Venus in palmistry. *Love.*

"Logan," she managed to say. "What are we doing?"

"Dancing around the edge of risk."

Her comfort zone started getting uncomfortable. Jen could even pinpoint its location. Under the breastbone, left side. "I don't do one-night stands," she said, more for her benefit than his.

His thumb continued to stroke her palm, making every nerve ending tingle. "Who says it has to end tonight?"

"Common sense," she said firmly. "We've only just met and I'm leaving for New Zealand tomorrow. Not to mention, I've just come out of a relationship..." Jen rattled on and he listened patiently. She sensed this man had the patience of Job when it came to getting what he wanted.

But he was sticking to his word. No pretty compliments, no promises, no telling her what she wanted to hear. The reminder quietened the reactive chatter in her head, allowed her to truly consider the possibility. Why *did* it have to end tonight?

The answer reverberated through her psyche, clear as a bell.

Because I don't trust my resilience.

Already, she experienced a deep connection with this man and such immediate susceptibility scared her. She needed to protect that small core of observer that had kept her safe since she was twelve years old. Her fear of abandonment ran too deep to take an emotional risk with a virtual stranger.

However thrilling his touch.

However much he seemed like someone she'd known all her life.

"I'm sorry, Logan." Jen cleared her throat. "I can't do this."

Logan squeezed her hand and released it. "Timing is everything," he said.

"Timing is everything," Jen echoed, relieved.

When Dave was killed, Logan had told the army psych that he'd mastered the fatalism that came with being in Special Forces.

As it turned out, he'd been like an animal hit by a car, still able to get up and run, even though mortally injured. For six months Logan had performed his duties as normal while the shock waves radiated through his psyche fundamentally changing his priorities.

Until one day he woke up and thought, *I'm done*. He didn't regret a single minute of his service, but he wanted to enjoy the outdoors without wondering whose sights he might be in. He wanted to stop being defensive for a living, to remember how it felt to be a civilian, to relax and be gentle and kind. He wanted to live the life he and Dave had joked about living when they 'retired.'

Rest in peace, bro.

Logan wanted his life easy, he wanted simple and Jen wasn't either of those things. She was a romance deportee avoiding another relationship; Logan was over quick affairs between tenures. She was resettling in New Zealand; Logan intended roaming Australia.

Complex and compelling, this woman could get addictive really, really quickly. And Logan set a high value on his freedom, he wouldn't relinquish it lightly.

When he'd left the service, he'd decided that if the universe wanted him somewhere it needed to provide a limo service. So he wouldn't coax Jen into an adventure she might regret, no matter how fascinating he found her. Why complicate his new life?

And yet…and yet.

She elicited tenderness from him like no one he'd ever met. When he looked into her eyes he saw a brave, funny, kind, sexy woman who deserved a man she could trust. He saw a woman who needed a champion, not in any physical sense—tonight she'd proved she could handle herself—but in an 'I've got your back' sense. He saw a woman he could love.

A woman still recovering from a relationship with a douchebag, unable to risk more heartbreak. Like she'd said, timing was everything. And theirs was out.

"It's late, Cowderella, well past midnight." There was no point dragging out the goodbye. Might as well make this easy on both of them. Standing, Logan offered

Jen his arm and a no-hard-feelings smile. "I'll walk you to your tent."

"Thanks for a lovely evening." Jen slid off the bar stool, untying the silk wrap from her waist and dropping it around her shoulders in preparation for going outside.

Briefly, she wished Logan had challenged her pragmatism with seduction. But only briefly. She'd never been one to delegate the tough choices. And she wasn't just protecting herself with this decision, she was protecting him. He deserved so much more than the doubts and fears she currently had to offer.

"I enjoyed it, too," he said. They made their way through the pavilion to the exit, passing a guy who'd fallen asleep at a table, one cheek squashed against the beer-soaked paper tablecloth, while his friends continued to party beside him.

Logan paused. "Do you need to phone your girlfriends for directions?"

"As long as we have a flashlight, I think I'll be okay." His consideration was sexier than any smoldering glance. "It's a five-minute walk, directly left of the picnic area."

"I have a light on my cell." He adjusted the jacket, briefly exposing a tanned pectoral muscle and tight male nipple. Throat suddenly dry, Jen forced her gaze to her surroundings.

Numbers had thinned to the die-hards, the dance junkies, and potential lovers still making their minds up about each other. Several woebegone faces suggested that not everyone's evening had lived up to expectations.

What about her and Logan? Would he try to kiss her goodbye? Her pulse kicked up. No, he'd said she had to initiate kissing. The choice was hers.

They stepped outside. Overhead, star clusters blazed

in cold brilliance making the floodlights dotted around the grounds look meager and lonely by comparison.

One woman's low angry voice carried in the quiet. "You *were* giving her the eye, Mark, I *saw* you." Life, Jen thought wearily, makeups, breakups, hits and misses.

Her pulse settled. She wouldn't kiss Logan. It would only make her sensible choice harder.

Arm-in-arm, four tipsy women in exquisite gowns, their elaborate hairstyles surrendering to gravity, meandered toward the entry gate ahead of them. One started singing an old Bonnie Raitt hit, "*Something To Talk About,"* and the other three raucously joined in.

She and Logan exchanged a smile before his gaze swept the grounds and passers-by in an assessment she guessed came automatically to him. His silence wasn't resentful or sulky as it might have been with another guy. Still, Jen felt oddly deflated. Turned out *not* risking a kiss and giving people something to talk about was much, much harder.

Under the thin wrap, she shivered.

"You're cold." Immediately Logan shrugged off his jacket, baring his torso. *Oh. Dear. God.*

Jen averted her eyes from temptation. "You'll be colder," she protested.

"I'll be fine until we reach your tent." He draped the jacket over her shoulders. The satin lining was blood warm and she felt it all the way to her bones, even through his shirt and Lily's wrap. Her next shiver was voluptuary. Oh God, did she *really* want to pass up a kiss with this man?

"Can you hand me my cell," he said. "It's in the jacket pocket."

As Jen retrieved it, her fingers brushed the cow tag and her heart shed another defensive layer. He'd kept it.

They passed through the entry gate where Logan nodded to the security guard. "I'll be back in ten minutes. I'm just escorting my friend home."

Friend. That's what she'd chosen to be, right? Yet an

inner voice protested. Her comfort zone, normally a refuge, was starting to feel like a panic room.

The pavilion's lights faded, the darkness engulfing them as they picked their way through the appearing clusters of tents and vehicles by a thin beam of cell-light. Logan reached back and caught her hand, Jen gripped it tightly. He must have cat's eyes, he seemed to maintain a sense of direction effortlessly. His fingers were warm and calloused, a lifeline in the pitch blackness.

"What kind of tent are we looking for?" Logan asked.

"A three-person dome tent," Jen said. "There's a white truck on one side of it and four green glow sticks along the other." Strategically placed by Ellie to stop anyone stumbling into the tent in the dark. "And guide us home," she'd said, what seemed like a lifetime ago. And suddenly Jen dreaded seeing the welcoming beacon.

She and Logan had been building to goodbye all evening and she'd thought she'd made it easy by holding back, keeping it casual. But even the part of her that was never trusting, never safe, yearned for more.

She had to kiss Logan, just once. The decision manifested as a revelation, lacking only the lightning bolt. She had to know his taste, feel his arms around her. Just once.

"Here we are." He stopped a few feet away from the tent. The glow sticks cast luminous green circles on the canvas.

Nervousness making her clumsy, Jen shrugged off his jacket. The wrap fell from her shoulders, she bent to fumble for it in the dark and Logan took the jacket and shone the cell's beam on the ground. The gold threads shot through the red silk gleamed.

Picking up the wrap, Jen handed it over. In the reflected light of the glow sticks, Logan was a dark silhouette, his face impossible to read. "Please thank Lily for this," she began, "and thank you again for a lovely evening." Her tone was too formal, too cold. Jen struggled for the right words to convey how magical it had been. "I'm so glad I met you," she finished lamely. Gah, she had a degree in marketing, could describe a Noosa sunset twenty inspiring ways. Why couldn't she articulate her heartfelt gratitude?

"I'm so glad I met you, too." His voice was low and husky.

As Jen mustered the courage to reach for him, Logan caught her shoulders and dropped a kiss on her cheek, a fleeting touch of his lips, over before she could register it. Abruptly, he released her. "Have a good life, Jen."

"Thank you," she said automatically. "You, too."

His hand brushed over her hair then he was gone. She watched the dancing beam of his cell until it disappeared, thankful for the darkness that hid her too-obvious devastation.

Why had she let him go? She had donned her professional hospitality persona and politely shoved Logan away. And in the process she'd deprived herself of the chance to… What?

Her fingers skimmed the place where his kiss had landed, trying to protect the lingering warmth as she replayed those last moments. He hadn't protested at the way she'd shut down the evening, had he? No. The wistfulness she thought she'd detected in his tone had probably been wishful thinking on her part. He certainly hadn't looked back, had he? No.

Guess she was the only one agonizing about their goodbye, Logan hadn't been affected at all. "And that's a good thing, a very good thing," she whispered, as she quietly unzipped the tent fly.

Ducking into the tent, she found it empty. Now wasn't that interesting? And a relief. Her emotions were all over the place and keeping a poker face in front of her sharp-eyed besties would be impossible. Exhausted, Jen switched on a battery lantern and dropped her shoes by the tent flap. They glittered. Oh, hell, in the brain freeze of their goodbye she'd forgotten to return Lily's stilettos.

And she still wore Logan's shirt, his bow tie.

Why hadn't he said anything? He was a details guy, organized like her...Unless he'd been as conflicted as she was. As torn, as confused, as blindsided.

There was only one way to find out.

Acting on impulse, Jen shrugged on the puffer vest on Ellie's sleeping bag and hastily slid her feet into flip-flops. Taking the lamp, she grabbed Lily's shoes and returned the way she'd come, using the pavilion's lights to fix her course.

She could be wrong, she could be setting herself up for more embarrassment and humiliation. So, she'd use the excuse that they'd forgotten to organize the return of his clothing. Except Logan was sharp, he'd see through that. Jen picked up her pace. Too damn bad. She had to know. For once, she was sidelining reason for instinct.

With the aid of the lantern, the walk to the gate didn't take nearly as long as picking her way in the dark. The security guard recognized her.

"Did you see which way Logan went? He forgot these." She held up Lily's shoes.

Grinning, he pointed toward the main pavilion. "I never took him for a cross-dresser."

"What...oh." Jen smiled. "Takes all sorts."

"Don't take too long," he added. "Technically, I shouldn't be letting you in."

"I won't."

She passed the rabbit, who'd given up his evangelism to chat up a girl of his own. Seeing Jen, he shook the basket playfully. Shaking her head, she waved and kept walking, searching for a glimpse of Logan among the stragglers.

Outside the pavilion, Jen stopped and spun around slowly. Even knowing she might end up looking foolish, she desperately wanted to see him one more time. Her gaze snagged on a tall figure. Logan was standing in the shadows beside the pavilion's entrance, caressing an item in his hand, his expression achingly regretful.

All Jen's doubts settled. *I was right to come.*

As she drew closer, she recognized her cow tag and stopped.

She'd had tantalizing glimpses of Logan's character throughout the evening, in the way he believed her capable of taking care of herself, in his sensitivity to wait until she asked for help, in his acceptance of her need to call the shots.

But what she hadn't appreciated until now was his willingness to fail. He wanted her. He wanted her as much as she wanted him. And in that moment, it struck Jen with blinding force that until ten minutes ago she'd never chanced failure.

She didn't apply for jobs she couldn't get, didn't put herself in situations she couldn't control—and the cow suit wasn't an aberration, she'd truly believed she could handle it. Karl had hurt, humiliated and embarrassed her but she hadn't loved him; hadn't burned for him, or any man. She'd never taken the temperature above lukewarm. No wonder Karl went back to his wife. He knew he'd at least experience passion.

She'd never felt that intensity. Until now.

"Logan."

He turned at the sound of her voice, his expression changing to friendly disinterest, a strategy Jen so often adopted herself.

"You forget something?" But she'd already seen behind the mask.

"Yes," she said, stepping closer. "You."

Very deliberately, very slowly she ran her fingers along his jaw, slid her hand behind his neck and drew his head down, until their lips were so close his breath feathered her cheek.

Logan stilled, waiting, and in that perfect moment of stasis, past and future fell away, leaving only this gift of present. Jen pressed her mouth to his, whimpering deep in her throat at the joy of finally touching.

She kissed him without conditions, holding nothing

back. Logan's arms closed tight around her, aligning her to the hard contours of his body. Jen slid her hands inside his jacket, her fingers brushing the warm satin of the lining before cleaving to the heat of his skin. *At last. At last.*

Mouth to mouth, tongue to tongue, soul to soul, they kissed, oblivious to the whistles of encouragement from amused passers-by.

"Get a ute," a male voice hollered.

The need for breath broke them apart. "Let's get out of here," Jen suggested.

Logan didn't ask if she was sure, because he didn't need to, she'd made sure her kiss told him everything. Arms around each others waists, they walked past the rabbit and toward the entry gates.

"Wait a sec." Jen steered them back to the bunny. Half-blushing, half-laughing, she held out her palm.

The rabbit assessed Logan and gave her two. "He looks like he's got stamina," he commented.

"He has," Logan said, and helped himself to a third. "But only for this woman."

Jen's blush deepened, but she ignored it, wanting to seize and celebrate every moment of their night together. "Mad skills?" she murmured provocatively as they walked away.

"That's for you to decide," he said and swept her into his arms for a hot, hungry kiss. *Mad skills*, was her last coherent thought.

CHAPTER 7

MOST PEOPLE CAMPED AS CLOSE as possible to the venue. Logan had done the opposite, with the result that his nearest neighbor was two hundred yards away. He'd chosen a boundary site near a stand of tall gum trees, and parked his truck as an additional privacy screen.

As he switched on a couple of LED strips hanging from the two-person tent's guy ropes, Jen saw a small circle of stones. They were filled with ashes, testifying to a previous campfire and he'd placed a fallen branch in front of it to act as a backrest. "I've been here a couple of days helping Lily out," Logan said, pulling a tarp out of his ute and spreading it over the log as a groundsheet before throwing down a blanket.

"You didn't stay with her?" Jen blushed, suddenly shy. Would they get naked here...now? What was she doing? One-nighters weren't her style, too raw, too rash.

"My sister is a wonderful person." Logan chuckled. "As long as you have a bolt-hole. Sit down," he invited. "I'll build a fire." He reached out and tucked a loose strand of hair behind her ear, his blue eyes open and warm. "Would you like a hot chocolate?"

"Love one," she said. This man understood foreplay. Her decision was rash maybe, but not sordid or desperate or alcohol-driven. And Logan was shy, too. It was in the way he looked at her, wonderingly, a little dazed. Neither of them had expected this rapport. Jen settled against the log, catching a pillow he tossed her to soften her backrest.

Curling her legs under her, she watched Logan move about his campsite, his movements efficient and unhurried as he lit a fire, boiled water on a small primus stove and spooned chocolate into a couple of tin mugs. "Sugar?"

"No. Thank you." Being here felt easy, right. She looked at the gum trees, admiring the bone white of the eucalyptus's trunk where the bark had peeled. In her state of sensual awareness she even fancied she could smell the astringent scent of gum leaves. Around the circle of smooth gray rocks, the red earth seemed to release its own glow as the kindling caught and the fire built.

When he carried over two mugs of steaming hot chocolate and sat beside her, she re-settled between his legs and leaned into his chest, still bare under the formal jacket.

"I expected your camp to be some kind of bivouac," she admitted, throwing the blanket across her bare legs. "But this is downright cosy."

His laugh was a low vibrating rumble up her spine. "I'm enjoying the luxury of *stuff* now I don't have to carry my home on my back anymore."

They lapsed into silence, a silence that was anticipatory and intensely erotic. They'd talked all evening and now...they didn't need to talk.

With Logan's warm body behind her, the fire's heat heating the rubber of her flip-flops, Jen savored her hot chocolate and watched bursts of sparks leap into the dark like escaping fireflies.

Their time together was so short. Yet inside the circle of flickering firelight, the circle of Logan's arms, it seemed as though time had stopped just for them. Even the raucous cries of party-goers sounded faint and faraway, on another planet, a different world.

Placing her empty mug beside her, Jen nestled her head on Logan's shoulder and gazed up at the night sky. "Can you track by the stars?"

"Both hemispheres." There was a smile in his voice. He kissed the tip of her ear.

"There's an app now," she teased. "I can point my cell at the sky—or could—and it tells me what stars I'm looking at."

"I have the pro version." Lazily, his calloused fingertips stroked the back of her hands as they rested on his thigh.

"I thought you'd disapprove, losing the old ways…"

"If it helps people get themselves out of trouble, then I'm all for it." Turning her palms up, he traced the fate lines down the middle of her palms to the light blue veins at her wrist and the sensitive skin of her inner forearm. Slid down to her wrist again.

"You do have an uncanny ability of showing up in the right place at the right time." Wherever he touched felt charged, tingling. Her pulse picked up. "When you're weighing up your next career, you might consider search and rescue."

Logan ceased his stroking. "That's a very good idea," he said.

"And you've got mad skills," she reminded him and felt his smile ruffle her hair.

"That's right." Slowly, unhurriedly, he freed her of the puffer vest and bow tie, unbuttoned her borrowed shirt and laid her body bare. Firelight danced golden on her skin and glinted off the diamanté clasp of her bra. Jen shifted, restless. She was already wet for him.

His erection pressed hard against the small of her back, but there was a delicious languor in his touch as he traced her collarbone, sliding his fingertips between her breasts to pause on the front clasp of her bra.

Jen lifted in invitation, but Logan moved on, stroking across each rib before his fingers fanned gently across her midriff. She sucked in a breath, her abdomen tightening, as his fingers dipped as far as the panty line before skimming a caress over the curves of her hips and waist.

His thumbs circled her nipples straining against their lacy cups, then moved to trace the smooth roundness of her shoulders, traveled down her arms to the inside of her wrists. Again and again, his hands repeated their unhurried glide across her heated skin and she found herself melting into him, surrendering to his assured touch.

When Jen thought she'd combust and murmured a protest, he unfastened the clasp of her bra, exposing her breasts to his gaze. She gasped at the erotic abrasion of his calloused palms as he ran them lightly over her nipples.

"My God," he said hoarsely, "you're a miracle."

It was too much. Trembling under an onslaught of emotion she never allowed herself to acknowledge, she closed her eyes.

"Jen," he breathed her name. "Be here with me."

She opened her eyes, turning her head to look up at him. His pupils reflected the firelight, the irises midnight blue. Beautiful. But it was his smile, tender and fierce, that made Jen's heart swell. Dammit, she was going to live this one night without second guessing tomorrow. *Tonight, I'm someone else, not me.*

"More," she said, shameless in need. "I want more."

"Soon." His voice was gravel and lust and tenderness. His palm slid down her stomach to her sex, his fingers lightly stroking through the lace. He cupped her there, letting her feel the heat and promise of him and a moan escaped her. "Logan." She'd never been so ready.

He slid his hand up and then under the elastic waistband, one finger sliding into the wetness to explore. Jen opened her legs wider.

"Oh, yeah, he whispered, "like that." Feather-light, he traced around her clitoris and her hips rose to increase the friction, wanting everything, wanting harder. Bending his head, he nipped her earlobe and obliged, one hand caressing her breast, teasing and rubbing her nipple, the other giving her what she needed, building desire until she shuddered into an orgasm as explosive as the sparks flying from the fire.

Freedom, she thought, this is how it feels. It had started with Clarabelle and not caring about appearances and ended with this sexual adventure with Logan. Was the intensity due to surrendering to herself, to him, or both? For now, Jen let herself fly.

And when spent, she floated down, he kissed her into life with savage sweetness—long, slow, deep kisses.

Inflamed by his passion, Jen turned to straddle him, half-naked under the gaping shirt. "Your turn," she whispered, pulling his formal jacket down his bare shoulders, just enough to entrap his arms.

Logan's pupils flared as he realized her game, his low laugh that of a predator, temporarily cornered.

"Be good," Jen ordered, amazed and delighted by her daring, reveling in the sense of power.

Logan relaxed against the log in tacit consent and she touched her teeth to the pulse in his throat, nipped gently and felt his breath gust on her hair in response. He'd made her feel so crazy good she wanted to leave him with an equally indelible memory of this idyll.

She kissed him until he was growling into her mouth, then suckled and bit and teased her way down his magnificent torso, intent on returning the pleasure he'd given her, hungry for every taste of him. Maybe she'd leave him with a few physical reminders of their night together. Part of her was amazed by her lack of inhibition.

If tonight was all they had, she was free to be whoever she wanted, and it was sexy, intoxicating to play captor with this strong, willing man.

When she finally freed his cock from his pants, it jerked in her hand and his balls were tight. "If you make me come—" he said hoarsely and she stopped his protest by lightly kissing the tip.

"We have all night," she murmured. Logan rolled his head back and closed his eyes, letting her have her way with him.

His cock was salt and silk-sheathed heat and she savored every inch, teasing and tormenting until he groaned, pushed her head away and came against her hand in thick, viscous spurts. When had she ever been so fierce, so demanding, so wanton? Never.

And after they cleaned up, she settled in his lap, grabbing the blanket and covering their half-naked bodies, while they held each other, damp and bare, skin to skin, listening to the fire crackle as it gnawed its way through the wood, sizzling when it hit eucalyptus resin.

"How many hours until dawn?" she murmured. Firelight danced across the planes of his face and gilded his smile.

"Enough."

Jen nestled into his body, feeling boneless. Her eyes closed. She forced them open. "We have to make every moment count."

Logan stroked her hair. "You're doing a damn fine job so far."

He smelled so good, wood smoke and spicy cologne and male. She nuzzled into his shoulder. "I might need a little time to recover."

"I think we both need to rebuild our strength." He picked up his half-empty mug and sipped it. Then kissed her. She tasted sugar and chocolate and hot, searching tongue.

When the kiss ended, Jen sighed, exquisitely happy. "Hold that thought."

CHAPTER 8

LOGAN FELT JEN SLIP INTO sleep. Her muscles loosened and grew heavy, slackness coming into her hold. Shifting slightly so her cheek nestled more comfortably on his shoulder he gathered her close. He finished his now cold chocolate and stared into the fire.

In the vast enclosing darkness, the flames were living things, flickering patterns on every surface within their radius.

He didn't know how the hell they'd make this work, only that this woman was his future. It was a rock solid certainty and his army mates would recognize his quiet conviction. Uncomplicated women were overrated— hell, they were probably boring.

He had wanted something this badly only once in his life, when he'd applied to the SAS and undergone the brutal application process that sorted the determined from the dreamers.

Jen was teaching him that a man could be both. Wanting the stars and moon and ready to travel any distance to get them.

It grew colder as the fire subsided to pulsating embers. Logan tucked the blanket tighter around them and felt the butterfly brush of Jen's lashes across his bare chest as she stirred.

Her hair flowed over his forearm, shiny as reflected water in the firelight. He hadn't even known he'd been in a drought, but now Logan understood that he'd closed off some of his emotions after Dave's death. For all his re-engagement with family and friends, he never stayed long enough to enter meaningfully into their daily lives.

Jen was making him reassess the value and beauty of commitment.

She shifted to look at him and he hardened to the promise in her shy smile. Feeling it, she stretched provocatively.

The urge to lift and resettle her on his cock became primal. She must have seen it in his expression and her eyes darkened in response. One kiss—frantic, passionate—and they were each fumbling for the condom, intent and serious. He reached for her almost blindly when he was done, lifting her higher into his lap. Her hands were frantic on his spine. "Hurry."

Her naked breasts were inches from his face and he tortured them both by pausing to nuzzle and suck and tease. Jen gripped his shoulders, then his hair, her bottom wiggling in his hands as she tried to squirm out of his grasp and impale herself on him. "Now, Logan," she ordered breathlessly, yanking his hair hard enough to hurt.

"Wild woman." Logan slid her home, the laughter catching in his throat as he sheathed himself in her slippery heat. God. Briefly, he closed his eyes and when he opened them he noticed hers shone with tears. His heart pinched. "Jen?"

She blinked furiously. "I'm so glad I said yes to one night with you."

He wanted to say, "This is just the beginning of us." Yet that seemed the exact wrong thing for her to hear, so instead he said simply, "Me, too."

He kissed her. Claimed her. And then she moved and claimed him.

They found their rhythm and it was wild and strong. With each rise and fall, her lovely bottom pressed against his thighs, and her firm breasts bounced. She was fearless and free and driving him to climax far too soon. Desperate, Logan caught her waist and slowed her down, needing to see her satisfied before he let go. It didn't— thank God—take long.

Hair flying, breathing labored, she gave a little cry and he kept her moving, wanting her to wring every last pleasure out of her orgasm. Her eyes met his, her mouth rounding in wonder and he let himself fly, coming hard, harder than he ever had before because he was giving up his heart.

Afterward, they crawled into his tent and wiggled into his oversized sleeping bag. He couldn't stop kissing her, her face, her lids, her eyebrows, her neck…her mouth. She unraveled under his caresses, returning them with a fervor that had nothing of caution and everything of a woman as dizzyingly blindsided as he was. This time he fell asleep first.

Logan woke up and she was gone. He hauled up on one elbow. His ears caught the ping of a guy rope followed by a muffled *ouch*. Crawling out of his tent, he stood. Dawn arced on the horizon, orange gold in a pale blue sky. But his focus was on the woman in flip-flops limping out of camp wearing his best shirt and her puffer vest. Naked, incredulous, he folded his arms. "You're kidding me."

Jen squeaked and spun round. Her expression reminded him of a diner doing a runner from a restaurant—well fed and guilty as hell.

"Seriously?" he said disgusted. "Not even a goodbye, a peck on the cheek or a nice fucking you?" He felt disgruntled, angry, hurt and scared all at the same time.

"I..." Jen hugged herself. "I hate goodbyes."

"So we're not even talking about the possibility of taking this further? Last night meant something only to me?"

To her credit, she struggled just a moment before saying softly, "No, it meant something to me too. And no, we're not talking about the possibility of taking this further."

"Why?"

"Because it was perfect," she said. "It was perfect and I don't want to ruin it."

Logan was nearly amused. "By getting to know me?"

"That's not the problem," she said quickly.

The dawn chill was raising goose bumps on his naked flesh; he ignored them. "By me getting to know you?"

"I wasn't myself last night, I was..." Jen lifted her gaze to the lightening sky as if seeking inspiration. "Uninhibited, passionate, adventurous and I'm not any of those things in my real life." Her gaze returned to his. "You'll only be disappointed."

"Great," he said. "Even more reason to pursue this. If I dislike the real you I won't pine. This is scary for me too, you understand. Maybe I'd rather get over you." He had a feeling he was seeing some of what Jen considered real about herself now. The defensive wall of polite, rational and careful.

Hell, she could be all those things, but not with him. "See, right now I still think you're resourceful, smart, funny and sexy. I also thought kind," he added, "but if that was true you wouldn't be hurting me by sneaking off like this."

"I...Don't be hurt." She took a couple of steps toward him, her face stricken. "This isn't about you, it's about me...my limitations. Last night was special and wonderful and I can't thank you enough for it. But that intensity...it won't last. It can't."

She wrapped her arms around herself—around his shirt—her dark eyes troubled. "I don't believe in love at first sight or fated mates or one true loves. I'm not saying there aren't exceptions to the rule—one in a million, maybe—but it doesn't happen to someone like me."

Logan frowned at her phrasing. "Why doesn't it happen to you?"

"I always believed because I didn't inspire it. Now I know it's because..." She met his gaze squarely. "I don't want it to."

"That," he agreed, "*is* a problem." If emotion scared her, then he had to be smart discussing this. A chance, that's all he wanted for them. "Let's talk this through sensibly," he said. "Logically."

She took a deep breath. "I'm not a risk-taker in relationships. And my recent experience with Karl has only reinforced that." She braced herself, as if for criticism.

Logan said, "Coffee?"

She blinked, and her shoulders lost a little of their defensive hunch. "You're going to be grownup about this."

"I'm going to try," he said wryly. "I'll go put pants on. You boil water for the coffee."

Her eyes flickered down his body and she swallowed. Immediately, his cock reacted. "No," he said, cupping his groin. "We talk. Unless I can fuck you into compliance? You can see I'm willing to make the attempt."

"I could lie and say yes." Jen's pained smile squeezed his heart. Jesus, did he really want to dive into a relationship? He'd just regained equilibrium and she was turning his life upside down. Did he *want* to get in deep with this woman?

"The primus stove is under the tarp." Logan returned to the tent.

Despite what she seemed to believe, some emotions couldn't be rationalized away. He wanted her, he was halfway in love with her and, God knows, yesterday he'd have laughed at the very idea. But he trusted his instincts and his instincts said, "Keep her." So he had to try.

The very fact she was running scared reassured him she felt the same way. She'd seen her dad turn into a frog and dated a few more amphibian types, so it would be tough recognizing a prince when he finally came along. Shaking his head at his thoughts, Logan fastened his jeans. He'd spent *way* too much time watching Disney princess DVDs with his tiara-wearing nieces lately.

Maintaining a relationship would be hard, she was right about that. It sure as hell wasn't going to be as simple as calling and saying, "Want to go on a date tomorrow?"

Distance aside, his relationships had been transitory, which meant his 'going steady' knowledge was negligible. He'd have to up skill on the fly.

They'd fast-tracked and now they had to go back and fill in the gaps. For example, did she like mushrooms? Logan knew two big things though: they'd stumbled into something special and Jen was a good person. She didn't want to hurt him. As he hauled on a T-shirt he thought ruefully, *Good, because I don't want to get hurt, either*. Already, the prospect of never seeing her again was painful.

He paused to collect his thoughts, to formulate some kind of strategy.

From what Jen had said of her childhood it was clear she hadn't been protected or cared for the way she'd deserved. It had taken her a lot of years to build up that defensive shell, he wasn't going to blast it open after one night—however much his male ego would like to think so.

Given the choice, he'd prefer to back off, give Jen space and woo her slowly. But they didn't have the luxury of time and he wouldn't pretend he didn't want her.

Which left him firmly wedged between a rock and hard place.

Jen watched Logan disappear into the tent and tried to work out if she was glad or scared that he'd heard her leaving. She decided both.

Last night she'd been loose and free and silly and brave because she'd believed she had nothing to lose. Nothing to sustain or maintain. The sex had been magical. The intimacy that went with it? Addictively terrifying.

She liked everything about this man, his thoughtfulness, his competence, his neatness—okay, *that* was sad—and his honesty. His quiet self-possession made Karl's silver-tongued charm seem try-hard.

But she was nothing if not a realist. Logan was above her pay grade, way above it. The way he'd talked about his family? This guy hit solidly in the normal range of the personality charts. Letting him see her screwed-up, complicated self…Jen winced at the thought.

No matter how romantic or special or extraordinary their evening was, they'd woken up in the real world with all the practical considerations that came along with it.

Deep in thought, Jen lit the primus, poured water from the ten-gallon container into a coffee pot, added grounds and set it to boil over the small gas burner.

Despite her views on fairy tale endings and love at first sight, secretly she'd always wanted one perfect, passionate night and he'd given it to her. A beautiful memory to marvel over when she was tired and lonely.

But once he got to know her? She'd blow it. An ice princess melting wasn't a pretty sight. Jen suspected she could be pretty needy if she let herself depend on someone.

She wasn't sure she could go through the crucible again.

In that pivotal year when her parents broke up and she'd found herself set adrift in a new country among strangers, she evolved strategies to cope. Ellie and Beth had shown her what was possible and, like a chameleon, she'd adopted some of their coloring—Ellie's courage, Beth's vitality.

Inside, she was still that child who'd huddled in a strange bed in a strange country, coming to the awful realization that even the people who most loved you could let you down. She'd toughened up, made a religion out of self-reliance...and in one single night Logan had nearly convinced her to break her vows. But in the cold, hard light of dawn she recognized their idyll for what it was—a lovely fantasy.

It wasn't real, because real meant she'd have to dismantle the hard-won independence she'd protected herself with over the past fourteen years.

The coffee gurgled in the pot, steam rising to merge with the soft grayness of early morning. The aroma was a reminder of her true habitat—corporate, urban, civilized. She'd chosen Karl because she'd thought she could merge her career with a personal life. And look how that turned out. Jen's nerves steadied. So did her resolve.

Logan ducked out of the tent, carrying a first aid kit. One glimpse of his rugged, thoughtful face and she was yearning all over again.

"What's the kit for?" Hopefully, to seal the crack in her willpower.

"Your bleeding foot."

Jen glanced down to see blood trickling over her foot. She'd stubbed her big toe on a guy rope sneaking out of the tent. It hadn't hurt until this second; she'd been too busy wrestling with inner torment.

"Thanks," she said, holding out a hand for the kit, but he'd turned away to pull a camp chair out of the ute tray.

"Here, take a seat, I'll tend it."

"You're bossy," she commented, pouring the coffee into mugs. "So am I. We'd drive each other crazy." Flippancy was the way to get through this. She didn't want him sensing her ambivalence.

"At least until we learned to compromise," he agreed. Dumping the chair, he opened a cooler and handed her some milk.

"I take my coffee black," she said, adding milk to his mug. "See how little we know about each other?"

"I take two sugars," he said, passing her a sachet and a teaspoon. "After a morning coffee, I swap to drinking tea. Please, sit. It's easier for me to clean the cut properly...unless you're a Yogi master?" There was wickedness in the glance he threw her and heat rose in Jen's cheeks thinking of some of the positions they'd managed.

Deciding her best approach was to remain slightly aloof, she sat. Logan crouched in front of her and opened the kit. She kicked off her flip-flop. *Aloof with dirty feet and sparkly toenail polish.* It seemed a lifetime since she and the girls had the manicures, Jen figuring she'd at least be well-groomed *inside* Clarabelle's hide.

Logan picked up her foot and examined it and she tried not to squirm. He didn't look up. "Ticklish?"

"A little," she admitted.

The stinging antiseptic he used to clean the wound took her mind off it. Jen concentrated on not moving. "And stoic," Logan said.

"Always." She looked at his dark head, bowed over her foot and a lump came into her throat. His eyelashes were gold-tipped and his hair would probably lighten under the sun if he grew it longer. The hint of a whorl at the nape of his neck reminded Jen of her earlier guess that it might be wavy. "Do you have curly hair?" she said hoarsely.

"Yeah," he said, intent on his work. "Like my mother."

The lump in her throat grew to Ayers Rock proportions. She would never meet his mother, or any of his other family.

The tip of his right ear stood a little farther out than the left. She wanted to rest her cheek against his crown and weep. And that wasn't like her, this onrush of tenderness, of need. She didn't do need. "Thank you."

He raised his head, still on his haunches and she got a shock of recognition looking into his piercing eyes. They seemed to see *her*, the person she kept hidden—the vulnerable, soft and wanting to be loved person. If she let herself get sucked into that…

He looked away to pick up his mug of coffee. "So you were going to run away with my shirt?"

"I was going to leave it for you at the information tent when I picked up Clarabelle. With a nice note, probably more civilized than *nice to have fucked you.*"

He pulled a face. "I was angry when I said that. We both know it meant a lot more."

Jen bit her lip. "My leaving isn't personal," she said, then realized how awful that sounded. "Hear how I keep putting my foot in it?" *This was why it was better to fade to black.* "Let's examine the facts." Facts she excelled at.

"Let's," he encouraged.

"How often would we see each other? I'm leaving tonight for New Zealand and you're of no fixed abode. You were the one who recognized I was in rebound mode so how can we be sure these feelings are real? You're a country boy and I'm a city girl. The job I'm taking on is for a three month contract, who knows where I'll end up? You're yet to decide what your next career will be before you can settle on a location." Briskly she itemized the many barriers to pursuing a relationship while Logan sipped his coffee and listened.

"Did you lie awake until dawn thinking about this?" he said when she'd finished.

"I woke up early," Jen said. *And worried at it for a good hour.*

"Let's keep this simple," he suggested. "What are you doing for breakfast?"

"What?"

"Let's meet for breakfast. We'll exchange last names and swap contact details. You can introduce me to your friends. We'll take this one hour at a time. But I'm not going to lie, Jen—you're making me feel things I've never felt for another woman…" He faltered, shrugged helplessly.

She held his gaze a few seconds and then glanced away, unable to bear the intensity building between them. "Logan—"

"You know what I liked best about last night?" Standing, he picked up the first aid kit. "It was easy. It was right." His gaze held hers, sincere, compelling. "We don't have to make it hard, Jen," he said softly.

"Except I can't help myself," she said, frustrated by both her reflexive neuroticism and Logan's refusal to be deterred by it. "Which is precisely my point."

He didn't answer immediately, unlocking his vehicle and dumping the first aid kit on the seat, packing away the primus and food supplies. Methodical, unhurried. Jen watched, unsure whether to be grateful or offended by the way he took the drama out of this discussion.

"Here's the deal," he said, glancing at his watch, as he returned. "I'll be at the breakfast tent in an hour, if you want to show up. Right now I need to check in with security and find out what Lily's volunteered me for."

She nodded, relieved. "And if *you* have second thoughts about meeting, I'll also understand."

He gave her an unreadable look. "Okay." Catching her face between his hands, he bent to kiss her, a light, tender brushing of lips. "I'm really hoping to see you soon," he said, turned and walked toward the venue.

CHAPTER 9

JEN TOOK ONE LAST, LONG look to imprint the scene. The big sky, a pale blue that would deepen to azure during the day, Logan's campsite, and the man himself, tall and strong, sexy and kind, walking away. Her vision blurring, she walked in the opposite direction, blinking hard. *No regrets*.

She had so few treasured memories that weren't tainted by what happened next. Her special outings with Dad, marred by coincidental meetings with a woman he told Jen to call Auntie Sonya.

Mum and Dad telling her nothing would change how much they loved her, before shipping her off to boarding school so they could slash at each other in the divorce court.

She and Ellie, acting as bridesmaids on Beth's happiest day in Vegas, only to watch their friend's heart broken by the man who'd sworn to cherish her.

Karl encouraging her to talk about her desire for a family a week before he said, "I've made a terrible mistake."

She couldn't take back all the experiences that had shaped her. Scarred her. And it was a shame because Logan was a wonderful guy, really wonderful. If she'd been the woman he met yesterday, ballsy and brave and optimistic instead of the scaredy-cat screw-up she really was, well, then she might have let herself be persuaded by his sincere conviction.

You needed luck to win at the game of love and she'd never been a gambler. Not with so many odds already stacked against them.

Jen stopped walking to wipe her eyes with the sleeve of his shirt. *Better to imagine how happy we could have made each other. Better than discovering how very much we can't.*

The sharp, short toot of a powerful horn penetrated her misery and she glanced up.

Hair damp from a recent shower, Ellie stood by the truck at their campsite, tent already packed up and the area cleaned. Clearly, she was ready to leave. No sign of Beth. Ellie's anxious features told Jen she wasn't the only woman on the lam this morning.

Straightening her friend's puffer vest over Logan's creased shirt, Jen opened her mouth to make light of her bedraggled appearance but burst into tears. Ellie's face crumbled too. The next minute the two of them were hugging each other half-sobbing and half-laughing as they assured each other that really they were absolutely fine.

"So." Ellie finally pulled away to wipe her face on her sleeve, her green eyes penetrating. "Best weekend ever?"

"Yes." With a resolute sniff, Jen straightened her shoulders. "I just have to get out of here before I ruin the best night of my life."

"That pretty much sums it up for me, too...and no, I don't want to talk about it."

"We're on the same page then." Jen scanned the surrounds. "So where's our third musketeer?"

Ellie frowned. "Didn't you get my text?"

"My cell's gone... Long story." Anxiety quickened. "Is Beth okay?"

"Physically she's fine," Ellie reassured her.

"Emotionally, I'm not so sure. As we speak, she's with Jonah Masters flying down to the coast to view a property he's thinking of buying."

"*The* Jonah Masters? From the headliner band?"

Ellie nodded. They looked at each other, their long friendship making words superfluous. *Another fucking music star, are you kidding me? Has she got a death wish? What happened to swearing off egotistical musicians? She's fragile and doesn't know what the hell she's doing.*

"I should have been here," Jen said.

At the same time Ellie blurted, "I should have tried harder to stop her."

Another shared look, then they both sighed. No one could dissuade Beth when she'd made up her mind.

"I *think* Jonah's a good guy," Ellie said tentatively. "And she knows him, he used to tour with Troy's band. But Beth's not ready to risk more heartbreak." Her gaze shifted beyond Jen to Rick and his mate's campsite, she swallowed hard. "Neither am I. Let's hit the road."

Jen's stomach plummeted. "Um…" She'd meant to shower, drop Logan's shirt off at the information tent and retrieve Clarabelle but Ellie clearly wanted to avoid running into last night's fling. Jen supposed she could always contact the organizers later.

Besides, her visceral reaction to the idea of leaving was a warning. If she didn't leave now, she might lose the courage to.

Ellie noticed her hesitation. "Oh, of course. You want to get dressed first."

"No, let's go," she said, opening the truck's door while she had momentum. "I'll change clothes when we stop for breakfast."

Settling behind the wheel, Ellie started the engine.

As they bumped across the rutted terrain, Jen caught herself turning to take one final mental photograph of the campground. Resolutely, she faced forward. "The last time I saw you, you were on the dance floor with

Rick's hot friend Jack. Is that why you don't want to see Rick? He gave you a hard time about hooking up with his best mate?"

"Rick is hotter," Ellie said in a small voice.

"Oh. My. God," Jen said, awed. Why else would fearless Ellie run? "Something happened with *Rick*."

"Yes," Ellie admitted, slowing to let another truck into the queue to the exit. "We did the dirty deed." She shifted down a gear, a little too forcefully. "And now I'm done with him."

Uh-oh. "He wasn't any good in the sack?" Jen used humor to gently gauge her friend's mood.

"No, he was good. Awesome, in fact. Mind-blowing." Grimly, Ellie stared into the distance.

The gates came into view, some hundred yards ahead and Jen's heart nearly arrested as she glimpsed a broad-shouldered security guard. Surreptitiously, she slunk down into her seat and peered over the dash. It wasn't Logan. Her heart lurched again, this time in disappointment, as she straightened. *You're doing the right thing,* she told herself.

Eyes on the queue, Ellie said dryly, "I'm guessing by the way you were cowering, that shirt you're wearing belongs to one of the security guards." She shot Jen an astute look. "Fill me in."

"His name's Logan…" Jen tugged his shirt over her knees and tried to make their encounter sound like a fun hook-up instead of the life-changing experience it was. "He suggested we meet up for breakfast to discuss what happens next." She kept her tone light. "What's the point if I'm leaving the country?"

"I left the country for six bloody years," Ellie said bitterly, planting her foot as the brake lights lit up on the vehicle in front. "And yet the moment Rick showed the slightest interest in me—" She refocused. "Sorry, I'm not helping, am I? What do you need me to say, hon?"

"Tell me he won't wait too long," Jen said. *Tell me*

he won't think less of me. She so badly wanted Logan to remember her as funny, feisty and brave.

"Text and tell him you're not coming." Reaching in her shirt pocket, Ellie tossed Jen her cell. "I'd rather not have this on me anyway, in case Rick calls."

You don't have to answer Rick's call. But Jen didn't say it. Sometimes friendship meant not stating the bloody obvious.

Activating Ellie's cell, she paused, dismayed, with her finger hovering over the screen. "I don't know Logan's number."

"Don't worry, he'll figure out you're not coming," Ellie patted her knee. "Did you tell him you're having second thoughts?"

"I did."

"Then you're covered. Tonight you'll be on the plane to New Zealand leaving behind any messy repercussions." She was clearly anticipating her next encounter with Rick. "You're *lucky.* You'll never have to see Logan again."

"Never," Jen repeated. It sounded so...final. And it was. She had no way of contacting him once she left these grounds. No cell number, no last name. What was his sister called again? Violet, Rose, Daisy? And why did it suddenly matter so much?

The truck edged its way to the front of the queue and with every yard gained toward freedom, Jen felt more and more trapped. They passed through the gates and she glanced at Ellie. Even the fearless one was running scared, so what chance did Jen have of making a relationship work?

But the rationalization died at birth. At least Ellie had *tried* following her heart. Even Beth was literally flying into another relationship. *I've never even left the starting blocks.*

"Stop!" The word exploded from her. Jen wrestled with the catch on her seat belt. "Stop the truck, I'm going back."

Ellie hit the brakes and pulled over to let other vehicles pass. "Jen, wait." Her green eyes were kind. "Take a deep breath."

Obediently, Jen sucked in oxygen.

"Are you sure?"

"No!" A strangled laugh escaped her. "I'm a total coward when it comes to love. But if I walk away, I'll regret it the rest of my life." She caught Ellie's hand. "Please say you understand."

Ellie returned a hard squeeze. "I do understand. I gave into my feelings for Rick for the same reason. It's not going to work out for us but..." Her voice cracked. "It was worth it. Now go."

Leaning forward, Jen hugged her fiercely. "Thank you," she said through a tight throat. Opening the door of the cab, she slid to the ground, and paused to fumble in the puffer vest's pocket. "I nearly took off with your phone."

"Hold onto it," Ellie said. "I'll stop for breakfast in Dubbo. If you change your mind in the next thirty minutes, leave a message at the Red Creek Cafe and I'll swing back and pick you up."

"Don't wait for me. I'm positive." If Jen was in, then dammit she would be all in. "That's how much faith I have in this guy." She glanced at her watch. Still forty minutes to make her rendezvous with Logan. "Wish me luck."

"Luck...but Je-en." Ellie grinned. "If you take your bag, you can shower and change. Maybe pretty yourself up a little?"

"How many years have you been waiting to say that?"

Ellie whooped. "Many, many, *many* years."

Grinning, Jen retrieved her suitcase from the ute tray then knocked on the side panel to let Ellie know she could go. Now she'd made the decision, Jen felt giddy. She was going to look so damn gorgeous that Logan wouldn't recognize her.

Pulling the retractable handle free, she jogged toward the camping ground, the suitcase bouncing erratically behind her.

Rick came running from the other direction. "Jen. Where's Ellie going?" The cowboy stopped, his puzzled gaze following the disappearing truck. "Is she coming back?"

Jen slowed but kept moving. "Sorry, Rick, she's heading home." However Ellie wanted to handle this, Jen supported her decision. "Can't stop to talk," she called over her shoulder. "I've got a date with destiny."

Logan was returning to his campsite with a walkie-talkie and security vest for his final security shift later that morning when he glimpsed Jen's profile. She was the passenger in a white truck that was edging forward to join the queue of vehicles leaving camp. He grinned. *City girl*. Probably heading to Dubbo for a decaf latte. The holler of greeting died on his lips as she twisted to glance anxiously behind her.

Her expression said it all. Regretful, determined...and fleeing.

Instinctively, he turned and walked in the opposite direction, getting the hell out of there before she spotted him and... What? Saw his disappointment, his shock, his disbelief? He'd been so confident she'd felt about him the same way he felt about her. Had he imagined their connection? The rightness of it? No. Fuck it, he hadn't.

Pivoting on his heel, Logan strode back toward the exit gates, determined to persuade, to cajole, to demand... What? He stopped, irresolute. He'd told Jen that meeting him for breakfast was her choice and clearly she'd made it. He'd told her no hard feelings and he was all hard feelings right now. He felt as if he'd been poleaxed. "Fuck!"

Raking his hands through his hair, Logan tried to think rationally. It was crazy, anguishing over a woman he'd barely met. Crazy to feel as though she'd yanked his heart out of his chest and stomped all over it. Jen owed him nothing. Hell, it was a *good* thing she was leaving. If she could do this kind of damage to him after one night, imagine how much devastation she could cause in a week.

"You okay, mate?"

"What?"

The woman was in her sixties, weather-beaten, kindly. He recognized her from the medical tent. "You're pacing, muttering. Did you do party drugs at the ball?"

"No," he said sharply. "I'm fine." When she looked skeptical he dredged for a smile. "It's... Everything's fine."

With a nod, Logan reverted to his original course, his campsite. If Jen wasn't feeling it, then he needed to respect that and let her go. He was stowing his tent into his ute when his cell vibrated in his pocket and he dropped it in his haste to answer and had to scrabble in the dirt. "Jen?"

"Logan, it's Tim, head of security. Listen, I know you're not due on shift yet but we've got some drunken idiots taking advantage of the emptying campground to spin their wheels. Eastern quadrant. Any chance you—"

"I'll be right there." It was a relief to trek farther away from the breakfast tent. Less temptation to be there for a meeting that would never happen.

He heard it first, the tortured squeal of brakes as the drivers spun in tighter and tighter circles, egged on by the wild enthusiasm of onlookers. Through the tents and vehicles clouds of red dust rose into the morning sky. The acrid smell of burning rubber bit into the back of his throat.

He passed a diminutive woman struggling to lift her

chiller into her station wagon and paused briefly to help. "They're bloody idiots," she commented, after thanking him. "There's hardly room to swing a cat, let alone—"

The crash hit like a sonic boom, resonating around the camp. Everyone packing up froze, staring in the direction of the sound.

Shoving the chiller into the trunk, Logan ran.

The two young thrill-seekers were lucky. One had a broken arm, the other mild concussion. Their old Holden V8 however…

While Tim oversaw the medical evac, Logan supervised the sedan's retrieval. A nearby camper used his Land Rover to winch it out of the shallow ditch and the rear bumper fell off with a thud. Closer inspection showed the trunk had crumpled over the left wheel hub. Someone would have to lever away the metal and change the slashed tire before it could be rope-towed to a garage.

Logan retrieved his automotive tool kit and set to work.

"You okay doing this?" Tim asked on his return from the med tent. "You're not supposed to be on shift for another couple of hours."

"I've got nowhere else I need to be," Logan said grimly. Metal groaned as he levered it free of the deflated tire. But he couldn't stop his mind endlessly rerunning his conversation with Jen this morning, going over what *he'd* said, what *she'd* said, trying to pinpoint where he'd gone wrong. Given how wary she was, playing it casual had seemed the best approach. Had he, instead, given her the impression he didn't care?

He glanced at his watch. Forty minutes past their meeting time. Even now he was making excuses, rationalizations... Maybe she hadn't been leaving. She said she'd arrived with two friends and he'd only seen one, maybe they were picking up the third? Or maybe his initial thought had been correct and they were headed out for coffee? *Hell, I can't stand this.*

Throwing down his crowbar he picked up the walkie-talkie and called Wayne. The goateed volunteer had been marching around on the first shift when Logan checked into the security tent.

"Mate, it's Logan. You still patrolling the pavilion?"

"Yeah, Logan, whassup?"

"Do me a favor? Take a look around and see if the woman who was in the cow costume last night is in the breakfast tent."

"Sure, hang on." A few minutes passed. "Not a cow in sight," Wayne reported.

Logan said patiently, "She'll be in civilian clothes today, mate."

"Jeez, Logan, I'm not sure I'd recognize her again. Brunette right? Short hair—"

"Her hair's long, but yeah, she's brunette. Dark-brown eyes." God, half the women here fit that description. How the hell did he describe qualities like resourceful, smart, funny and sexy?

"Hang on," Wayne said. "I'm doing a walkabout. I didn't see her out of that cow costume. What kind of build are we talking?"

Logan found himself air-shaping Jen's curves. "Slim," he said. "34, 26, 34."

"That's specific," Wayne said suggestively.

Logan didn't reply and the guard took the hint. "It's pretty crowded here, lots of couples—"

"She'll be alone."

"Not many of those... There's one. Nope, blonde... Ha! And pregnant. Okay...I see a brunette—a real looker—but she's not ringing any cow bells with me." He snickered. "And her hair's short, not shoulder-length. Wait a minute...it's in some kind of bun thingy. She looks like she's waiting for someone. Kinda anxious, keeps checking her watch."

Logan's hand tightened on the walkie-talkie. "Go ask her name."

"Walking toward her. Whoa! She just threw herself into some dude's arms. Some guys get all the luck."

"They sure do." Logan bowed his head. "Well, thanks anyway."

"If it's urgent, I could put an announcement out over the speakers?"

Jen was at least eighty miles away by now. "That's okay, mate, it's not important. I loaned her a shirt and she mentioned she might return it."

"I can check at the information desk for you."

"No, don't worry about it." By tomorrow Jen would be over nine hundred miles away in New Zealand.

"I'm five steps away from the information desk now. Hang on a minute and I'll check."

Logan feigned surprise when no shirt materialized and thanked Wayne for going above and beyond the call of duty.

"The cow costume is still here though," the other man said eagerly, "I'll drop it by your campsite."

"Don't both—"

"No trouble. The team's gotta stick together."

Logan hooked the walkie-talkie over the Holden's wing mirror and picked up the crowbar. Stopped thinking, stopped feeling. Concentrated on doing.

Thirty minutes later, he returned to his camp to drop off his tools and grab clean clothes for a shower, ignoring Clarabelle who'd been slotted under his ute, next to one of the rear tires. When he returned from the shower block, he texted his sister.

I'm ready for food, want to meet up?

Sure. Breakfast tent. Ten minutes.

As he left he picked up Clarabelle and had to resist the urge to bury his face in her mangy, beer-splattered hide. "Looks like we've both been ditched," he said.

Passing a jumbo bin, Logan opened the lid and tossed in the cow costume. Clarabelle's eyes bounced around reproachfully.

"Yeah, well, life *is* hard," he rasped. "Get used to it." Shaking his head—why the hell was he talking to a piece of fleece?—he dropped the lid and walked away.

CHAPTER 10

FINALLY, SHE WAS TURNING HEADS for the *right* reasons. Jen threw her wolf-whistler a grateful smile before hesitating at the breakfast tent's entrance to hand-press the last wrinkles out of her lacy white T-shirt.

She hadn't packed knock 'em dead clothes, but her fitted khaki shorts did great things for her legs, her sandals were strappy and her make-up flawless. Her hair had gone frizzy after crouching to dry it under the hand-dryer in the women's shower block so she'd twisted it and pinned it into a chignon.

Rick had phoned while she was still in the shower, forcing her to scramble for Ellie's cell. He'd taken a moment to respond to her greeting.

"Jen... What are you doing with Ellie's phone?"

"I can't talk right now, Rick. Date with destiny, remember? Maybe later."

She glanced at her watch—five minutes early. Super Jen returns, she thought happily. Straightening her shoulders, she took a deep breath and entered the tent, wheeling her suitcase behind her. The place was packed, though compared to yesterday the mood was subdued. Most people wore sunglasses to hide the ravages of a big night.

Jen scanned the tables, then the benches on either

side. Her gaze settled briefly on a couple of pairs of broad shoulders then moved on. Logan wasn't here yet...unless there was another entrance?

She slowly walked the length of the tent twice. Nope. Only one entrance. Checked her watch. Bang on their meeting time. Parking her suitcase where she could keep an eye on it, Jen joined the queue at the coffee cart.

About to order, she remembered Logan preferred tea later in the morning. With milk, or without? What about sugar? She switched the order to hot chocolate instead, smiling as she remembered the last time they'd drunk it.

Shouldering her handbag, she accepted the paper cups, paid the server and maneuvered slowly and carefully through the crowd toward her suitcase, determined not to spill a single drop over herself. Today, he would see her perfectly groomed.

Settling near the entrance, Jen sipped her coffee and amused herself by spotting the new hookups. Oh, they were definitely one—hands all over each other. The older couple she'd glimpsed on the dance floor last night strolled by, hand in hand and she nearly called, "Hey, I'm a believer now," but that would be nuts. It was far, far too soon to call odds on her relationship with Logan. Still, she glowed.

Ten minutes passed. Logan's hot chocolate grew tepid in her hand. He must have gotten held up. Jen finished drinking her coffee and dropped the paper cup into a nearby bin. Her faith in him was so strong, it was thirty-five minutes before she even considered that he might not be coming.

She swatted the notion away. There must have been an emergency he couldn't get out of. And he knew she didn't have a cell. Another ten minutes passed. The fingers holding his drink grew stiff and she switched hands. The first chill of doubt entered her heart.

Logan was resourceful. If he was caught up in an incident and couldn't get hold of her, he'd send someone to tell her what was going on.

What if all her wavering had made him decide not to bother? No, he was keen, really keen. And dogged and determined. The guy she knew wouldn't make that assumption. Jen closed her eyes. *The guy she knew.* Wow. That would be the same guy she'd met less than twenty-four hours ago.

Still she sat there, periodically swapping his drink between her increasingly cold hands, believing. Until finally...she couldn't. *He's not coming.* The realization anchored painfully in her stomach. She pressed a hand to it. *He's not coming.*

In some bleak, black way, Jen thought numbly, this could be funny. She'd talked herself *into* meeting Logan, having talked Logan *out* of meeting her. By telling him all the reasons it wouldn't work, she'd clearly revealed enough of her real self to scare the poor guy away. One day she'd laugh at this. One day. Forcing her brain to work, Jen retrieved Ellie's cell and found the last caller's number.

Rick picked up on the first ring. "Ellie?" he said eagerly.

"No, it's Jen with Ellie's phone," she reminded him, her voice perfectly steady. "Have you left for Coolibah yet?"

"Why, do you need a ride?"

"Yes, please." Carefully, she tipped the cold chocolate into the potted plant by the entrance and tossed the empty cup into the trash. "When are you planning to leave?"

"In a few minutes. I'll meet you at my truck."

"Can you swing by the breakfast tent instead?" She'd gift Logan every last second chance to give her a miracle.

Rick arrived ten minutes later, carrying a bacon and egg roll. She must have interrupted *his* breakfast. A smile was beyond her, so Jen waved to get his attention. She'd wept once today, she wasn't going to do it again. Better to have tried and failed... Oh, fuck off. Later she'd pat herself on the back for her courage, right now she felt bruised and bloody.

As she walked toward Rick, she noted the defensive hunch to his shoulders and recognized a fellow sufferer. Burning up the swag with Ellie clearly hadn't resolved anything for him, either.

For the first time, Jen understood why he'd held back for all these years. It was safer that way. Why open yourself up to a world of pain?

Ellie's cowboy held out the roll. "Thought you might be hungry." *So much for my poker face.* Rick's thoughtfulness in offering comfort food when he was hurting, too, was the last straw. Tears started streaming down her cheeks. Jen stared at him helplessly.

Rick rescued the roll, tucked it into his jacket pocket, and patted her back. "I'm guessing your date with destiny didn't work out."

"He stood me up." Hating crying in public, Jen hid her face against his chest. She struggled to contain her sobs, to let the poor guy off the hook.

Rick—bless him—stood stoically under the assault. "Maybe he had a good reason for not showing up," he offered, but Jen heard his lack of conviction.

He did... Me. She wept into his gray-blue shirt. "I feel like such a fool. It took all my courage to put myself out there."

His arms tightened around her. "You're not a fool for taking a chance, Jen, and hell, you're right. There is *no* excuse for leaving you hanging." He added grimly, "Either someone's important to you, or they're not."

And I wasn't important enough. As tough as the realization was, it had the same bracing effect on Jen as a bucket of cold water. *Okay then,* she thought. *Okay.* She released her death grip, wiped her eyes. "You're absolutely right."

"Ready to leave?" he asked gently.

With a last sniff, Jen nodded. "Thanks for letting me cry on your shoulder." She managed a watery smile.

"Ellie's right. You're one of the good guys." His mouth set at the mention of Ellie's name. He pulled the squashed roll out of his jacket pocket and offered it to Jen again.

It was the last thing she wanted but she owed him, so she accepted it and took a big bite. "I appreciate the food."

See, I'm fine now. We're both fine.

Like either of them believed it.

He picked up her bag and she stopped him. "One second."

Opening a side pocket, Jen pulled out Logan's folded shirt. "I need to run this over to the information desk so I'll meet you at the truck."

She watched him set off toward the campground, steeling herself for her final goodbye. At the information tent, she borrowed a pen from the weary volunteer staffing the desk and tried not to chew it, while she considered what to write. In the end, she kept it simple.

Guess I talked you out of it. Hey, I understand second thoughts. Jen took a deep breath and let resentment go. *Thank you for last night, rebound guy and have a wonderful life. Jen.* Folding the note she scrawled on the outside: *For Logan, on security.*

As Jen walked toward Rick's truck, she felt better. It hadn't worked out but she'd been brave, taken an emotional risk and that was something to celebrate. Right now, it was small comfort, but it was *some* comfort and she wasn't going to let morning-after heartbreak ruin the most magical experience of her life.

She liked the person she'd become last night and that woman would make an appearance more often. By the time she was eighty, she'd be an eccentric spinster with a vibrator and a single figure golf handicap. Lips quivering in a wobbly smile, Jen wiped the tears spilling from her eyes. *Go me.*

If misery loved company, Rick fit the bill perfectly,

neither of them talking much as they began their four hour drive to Coolibah.

Rick wasn't a guy who asked for advice in matters of the heart, and Jen had just patently demonstrated how unqualified she was to give any. She didn't know why her most intrepid friend had run from this decent man, but she was going to find out because—dammit—*someone* had to have a happy ending.

And Beth might be rushing into another relationship before she'd let herself heal from the last one. It seemed to Jen that her friend needed a spell as the star act in her own life first. As she'd told Logan in the bar, timing was everything.

And Jen had made her move too late.

"Are you even listening to me?"

Logan refocused on his sister's frown. "Of course I am," he hedged. "You were just telling me how grateful you are for all my compulsory volunteering."

She sat back, popping the final morsel of croissant into her mouth. "No," she said between chews. "I was just thanking you for re-volunteering for next year's ball."

"Nice try, sis. I'm not *that* distracted." And he wouldn't be returning, not now. Not ever. He could barely sit still through breakfast. He looked at the scrambled egg congealing on his plate, and pushed it away.

Lily said quietly, "What's wrong, Logan?"

"A cow flicked her tail at me and I fell in love," he quipped. "Unfortunately, she wasn't equally mooo-ved."

"Your puns are terrible," she said, reassured. He'd told her the date with Jen was fun, nothing more. "So you're heading to Penny's next?" Their oldest sister lived in Melbourne.

What he really wanted to do was drive into the desert and howl at the moon for a few days but the army had taught Logan to do his duty. "That's the plan." He was a guy for fuck's sake, he shouldn't be moping because a pretty woman only wanted a one-night stand.

"Hey, Logan, this got dropped off at reception for you." Swaggering over, Wayne nodded officiously to Lily before handing Logan his folded dress shirt. "There's a note tucked inside the pocket."

Conscious of two curious gazes, Logan said casually, "Thanks, mate. Sit down, have a coffee. Hell, let me get it for you."

Pushing up from the table, he headed to the coffee stand. With his back to them, he opened the note. *Guess I talked you out of it.* His eyes widened. Incredulous, Logan scanned the rest of the note and went straight to the table. "You said she wasn't there," he accused Wayne. "That's what you said."

"She wasn't," Wayne was helping himself to Logan's discarded breakfast. Chewing a rasher of bacon he added thoughtfully. "Unless she was undercover again. There was this rabbit—"

"You went to the information desk while we were on the phone, there was nothing left for me."

"Nope, so I checked again as I was coming off shift. I like to be proactive with these things," he said to Lily. "Razor-sharp, that's—"

"So Jen was there," Logan said impatiently. "She had to have been!" He felt sick and elated at the same time, torn between strangling Wayne for missing her and kissing the guy for checking the information desk again.

"So about that coffee," Wayne hinted.

Logan looked at his watch, making calculations. "She's probably two hours' drive from here by now." He didn't even know in which direction. "And she's leaving for New Zealand tonight."

"I thought you said it wasn't serious," Lily said indignantly, but Logan barely heard her.

"The cattle station she was staying on was four hours' drive...north." His memory coughed up the detail under intense mental pressure. Pulling out his cell, Logan searched the internet for a state map and stared at the vast swathe of territory that constituted north. "North-east, north-west or north-central?" he muttered.

"I'll get us all coffee," Lily said. "I think we're going to need it."

Wayne watched Logan, fascinated. "So, you and the cow on a mission?" he said through a mouthful of food.

"Yeah," Logan said absently, sinking into his chair. "If she's flying to New Zealand, I could go to the nearest international airport and hang around departures." He highlighted airports on the map. "Except if I can't pinpoint her locale, it could be either Gold Coast or Sydney airport." He dropped the cell and gripped his hair in his hands. "Fuck!"

"You should have tagged that heifer when you had the chance," Wayne joked.

Logan lifted his head to stare at him.

Wayne stopped mid-chew. "Shit, mate, I didn't mean any disres—"

"You," Logan said reverently, "are a genius." He dug a hand in the pocket of his jeans and pulled out the cow tag he'd rescued from his suit pants. Hallelujah, it had a number on it. "You might even have to be best man at our wedding."

Lily returned with a tray holding three coffees. "I thought you said it wasn't *serious*."

"This number," Logan said, thrusting the cow tag at her. "What's it for?"

"Guys and gals can match up their numbers for a dance. It's an icebreaker."

"So it's not registered to the person allocated the ticket?"

"Nope, sorry."

His momentary hope died. Logan CPR'd it to life again. There had to be a way. "You have a list of people who bought tickets though, right? Addresses, phone numbers?"

"Yes," Lily said, "but—"

"No buts," he said. "Jen mentioned one of her girlfriends bought the tickets. It made sense that it was the local, the rancher who'd suggested the ball. I'll ring every female with a rural address living three to six hours' drive north of here."

"For real?" Wayne queried. "You're talking six to seven hundred kilometers across the state. And every little town in between."

Logan already knew it was a long shot. He turned to his sister. "How would you describe me?" he asked. "Steady, reliable, pragmatic, unromantic?"

Lily nodded. "All those things."

"Me, too," he said. "And yet, here we are. Now show me those lists."

Turned out mostly women bought the tickets—he should have expected that. Logan culled numbers down to a hundred. One hundred women to phone. He made a start as he packed up camp.

"Hi, my name's Logan Turner and I'm trying to find a woman I met at the ball. Do you have a friend named Jen?"

Two and a half hours later he was refilling the ute's tank at a gas station in Dubbo, hoarse and increasingly desperate. He'd left messages for fifteen women and talked to twenty-five, many of them inclined to chat. Some thought it funny, some romantic, some had practical suggestions—such as a lonely hearts ad in New Zealand's leading newspaper.

Two had complained that he shouldn't have been given their number, which was true, but were reassured when he told them he'd been cleared for security detail—also true. Jen had left an item behind, he said, without specifying that it was heart-shaped, weighing about 320 grams. That satisfied them.

But he still had sixty calls to go.

So when his cell rang with an unknown number as he replaced the pre-pay gas pump, Logan hesitated. Too often it was someone he'd already called, checking to see if he'd tracked Jen down yet. Walking away from the forecourt, he picked up just before it went to message. "Hello?"

"Is this Logan, the security guy who stood up one of my best friends?"

He stopped dead. "I saw Jen leaving early in a truck. It looked like she was keen on making a fast getaway. My mistake."

Silence.

Holding his breath, Logan waited.

"No," the female voice conceded. "You were right. She was doing a runner, but she changed her mind."

"So...is she there? Can I talk to her please? Sorry, what's your name?"

"Ellie. And she's not here to talk to. My father took her to Tamworth airport for her connector flight to Sydney and then New Zealand. I'm guessing she told you she was leaving?"

"She did." He strode to his truck, screwed the cap on the gas tank, slammed the cover shut. "What time is her flight from Sydney to Auckland?"

"Seven."

Climbing into his vehicle, he checked the clock on the dash. It was a five-hour drive to Sydney airport. It was tight, really tight. He started the engine and hit the highway east. "I know Jen lost her cell, but is there any way you can contact her?"

"She's phoning me from Sydney Airport."

"I'm going to try and get there before she leaves," he said.

"And you're still in Dubbo?" Ellie said wonderingly.

Logan grinned. "No, I'm a mile outside Dubbo. Listen, if she phones, don't tell her I'm coming in case I don't make it. I've disappointed her enough for one day."

"And if you don't make it?"

"I've always wanted to visit New Zealand."

"Wow." Ellie whistled. "Maybe this will work. I'm sorry I didn't check messages earlier but I'm dealing with my own romantic drama."

"Fingers crossed for both of us," he said. "Um, Ellie, one more thing...it's kinda embarrassing. What's Jen's last name?"

There was laughter in her voice. "Tremaine. I'll phone you again if I can help further. Good luck, Logan."

"Thanks, I'm gonna need it." Ending the call, he put his foot down.

CHAPTER 11

JEN USED THE LAST OF her change to call Ellie from Sydney Airport's payphones. "I miss you already, bestie. Did you manage to resolve anything with Rick?"

"I'm wrangling him into shape." There was laughter in Ellie's voice. In the background, Jen thought she heard a husky protest.

She grinned. "I'm interrupting… I'll call you from New Zealand."

"No, wait! I have got news but first things first. Your plane hasn't been delayed by any chance has it?"

"No, why would it?"

"No reason."

Jen stuck her hand over her free ear to block out the chatter bouncing off the concourse. "I'm just about to go through security. There are some good duty-free stores on the other side and I desperately need a new cell."

Then she'd find her departure gate early, and try to doze until boarding. She'd barely slept in thirty-six hours. And she could do with the temporary oblivion.

"The phones are way better priced in the duty-free stores in New Zealand," Ellie said. "Honestly, I'd wait until you get to Auckland."

"How would you know?"

"Um… Beth just told me."

"Oh my God, she's back? Put her on the extension. How did her night go with Jonah Masters?"

"Actually, she phoned to say she was staying another night and coming home tomorrow."

Jen said slowly, "The price of cell phones in New Zealand's duty-free stores arose in a conversation with Beth in which she informed you she was spending more sexy times with one of the hottest guys in music."

"Apparently, he's a bargain-hunter," Ellie said. "And don't go through security yet," she added hastily before Jen could speak. "I want you to do something that will cheer you up, and I *know* you need cheering up, Jen, so don't deny it. Go sit in the arrivals area and watch all the reunions. It's a really cool way to pass an hour. You've still got plenty of time before you need to go through customs."

"It's a long walk to the arrivals hall."

"Perfect for avoiding deep vein thrombosis."

"Okay, sweetie," Jen humored her friend. This unaccustomed ditziness of Ellie's had to be tied to Rick. "We're nearly out of time. Tell me your news."

"First, promise you'll do as I ask." Ellie coaxed. "Please? I want to think of you in Australia as long as possible."

"I've run out of coins. We're going to be—" The dial tone buzzed in. Jen hung up, shaking her head. "I'll only cry," she muttered, but shouldered her handbag and obediently wandered over to arrivals.

Within five minutes of settling into a seat in front of the arrivals gate, her throat was tight; within ten, she was blinking away tears. But it was a catharsis of sorts. Even on one of your worst days, it was good to be reminded that there were still dozens of families, friends and lovers reuniting. "I will get past this," she promised herself, watching an elderly Chinese couple meeting their grand baby, possibly for the first time, their wrinkled hands passing tenderly over the infant's downy head.

The young woman sitting beside Jen shrieked and leaped to her feet. She hurtled toward a laughing backpacker who shrugged off his backpack and opened his arms to her. Picking her up, he twirled her in a circle, nearly taking out the Chinese grandparents.

Jen grinned through tears. Someone sat beside her and, embarrassed by her second-hand sentimentality, she turned away.

"I'm sorry I doubted you." Logan said. Jen swiveled in her seat to gape at him. "I didn't show for breakfast because I saw you leaving this morning."

"Wait." Her brain struggled to connect the dots. "How?"

"I thought you'd changed your mind about meeting me."

"I mean, how did you get *here*."

"I drove from Dubbo."

"Today?"

"Yeah."

She swallowed hard. "For me?"

"Yeah."

"Why would you go to so much trouble?"

His eyes were very blue, very tender. "For the same reason you got out of the truck."

It felt like her heart might burst. "I don't believe in love at first sight," she managed to say.

"It wasn't first sight," he reminded her patiently. "Remember? I checked out your friends."

"Oh yes," she said, relieved. Mentally, she raised her arms to the dive position, took a deep breath. *Don't look down.*

"And it's impossible to fall in instalove with a cow," he said.

"You're right," she said, her gaze clinging to his. Looking down wasn't so hard.

Logan said gruffly, "We have, maybe, ten minutes before you go to departures. Are we really going to waste it dis—"

She tumbled sideways into his lap. Grabbing his shoulder with one hand for balance, pulling his head closer with the other for glory, Jen kissed him as if her life, her future depended on it. The cheerful raucousness of the terminal and the smirks of the onlookers faded. Nothing mattered except the feelings she revealed for him. And the answer he gave her. *You. Me. Real.*

They broke apart to a smattering of applause from the rows behind and grinned at each other.

"I feel like I've known you all my life and I know nothing about you," she said giddily. "You know nothing about me. How is this even possible?"

"I don't know, only that it is."

"I have to go," she said.

"You have to go. You're starting a new job tomorrow." Catching her hands, Logan pulled Jen to her feet and into his arms. "My last name is Turner and I want the contact numbers of every close friend and relative you have."

"And me for you. And I'm Jen Tre—"

"Tremaine, Ellie told me."

"Ellie…how? Never mind." She kissed him again. "We'll make this work."

"We'll make this work."

He bent to pick up a large plastic carrier bag on the floor next to the seat he'd just vacated. "I bought you a present."

Looking inside, Jen met Clarabelle's crazy eyes and laughed, delighted. "Thank you for keeping her safe. I hope Ellie can part with her because I can't give up the cow responsible for bringing us together."

"I had to go back for Clarabelle for the same reason," Logan said. With a groan, he pulled her into his arms again for another lingering kiss. "Besides, she's the perfect date for Wayne."

Jen cupped his face, marveling at how much she felt for this man. "Wait…where does Wayne fit into this?"

Turning his head to kiss her palm, Logan grinned.

"I'll tell you when the time's right." He glanced over her shoulder. "Speaking of which…"

Jen turned to the arrivals and departures board. "Boarding begins in fifteen minutes and I still have to clear security." Clasping hands, they jogged toward her terminal, Logan carrying Clarabelle.

Her heart full, Jen shot him a sideways glance. "The moment I didn't fall in love was when I saw you standing all alone and brave with my ear-tag."

Logan stopped jogging. "Hell, if this is pity," he began, mostly joking.

"And recognized a kindred spirit." Undeterred, Jen yanked on his hand to keep him moving. "I wanted to be your friend…and your lover." Still jogging, she started to lose her breath. "I wanted to say…'I get you… And I'm here for you'… Ack, and now I'm…*leaving*."

Logan laughed. "The moment I didn't fall in love was when you came out of the Portaloo wearing my shirt, all feisty and brave and trying not to cry."

"Oh, God, Logan." Jen stopped to wrap her arms around his neck. She would probably never get her breath back around this man. "Who knew," she said shakily, leaning her forehead against his, "that it could be this easy."

"Screw time and place," he told her fiercely. "If it's the right person, you *make* it work. What are you doing next weekend?"

"Working," she said ruefully. "But during the week I have days off and I'm eligible for employee discounts on hotel rates." She fumbled in her bag for a notebook, ripped out a couple of pages and handed one to Logan with a pen. "Phone numbers…and give me your cell number. And Lily's cell."

"I want both your parents' and the hotel you'll be working at," he said.

Using each other's shoulders as a hard surface, they hastily scribbled down contact info.

"Passengers on Flight NZ26 to Auckland should be

making their way to the departure gate for boarding."

"I'll phone you," Jen said, "as soon as I get to Mum's." They exchanged pieces of paper then started running in earnest. "We can't lose these."

"I'd find you," he promised. They reached the departure area where an official was channeling departing passengers toward security. Logan gave her Clarabelle. "I will always find you. Shit, that sounds stalkerish." He ran a hand over his hair. "I need practice with this stuff."

"No, it's perfect." Laughing, Jen pulled him close for a last, fervent kiss.

He smiled against her mouth. "We're perfect together." Reluctantly, he released her. "See you soon, Cowderella."

"You can bet on it." Smiling into his eyes, she touched his cheek then turned and hurried toward passport control, the bag carrying Clarabelle's head bouncing off her thigh.

Jen didn't look back. She didn't have to.

She trusted Logan to follow.

Three months later

At 4:00 p.m. on a wet Monday the plush house bar at the Auckland Grand Hotel was sparsely populated. Jen shifted nervously on her bar stool, checking her watch for the fifth time and mentally recalculating times for airport processing, transfer and hotel check-in… He was late.

The barman pushed a glass of red wine across the honey-colored kauri top. "Medicinal purposes. My treat."

Jen smiled gratefully. "You're a lifesaver."

He inclined his head and the trio of overhead lamps gleamed off the gel he used to keep his unruly dark hair civilized for work. "I aim to please."

Jen took a swig of the wine, barely noticing its quality. "I don't have any idea how to approach this conversation," she confided, setting it on the coaster he'd provided. "Do I tell him to hope? Keep waiting? Or to give up and get on with his life?"

"You'll know the right decision when you see him." The barman's gaze lifted, but Jen had already heard the approaching footsteps.

She spun on her stool and stood, smoothing down her working uniform of pencil skirt and white blouse. It didn't help her nerves that she had a massive fan girl crush on the Rowdy Boys lead singer.

"Mr Masters." Jen offered her hand to the man in unrequited love with one of her best friends. "I hope you enjoy your stay at the Grand." The band was touring New Zealand and he'd specifically asked to meet Jen on his arrival.

They both knew why—Beth.

"Call me Jonah." His eyes and hair were the color of expensive cognac. And yet this beautiful man's palms were as damp as hers. Jen looked past his famous face and saw strain, heartache and the need for hope.

Her nervousness dissolved in a rush of empathy. "What would you like to drink?"

"A beer would be great." He glanced past her to smile at the bartender. "Whatever the best local brew is, mate."

"I'll bring it over."

"Thank you," Jen said. Exchanging a last look with her confidante, she picked up her wine and gestured Jonah to a private booth in the corner. The elderly couple poring over tourist brochures by the fire were unlikely to recognize him, but there were plenty of other guests who would. Fans had been gathering outside the hotel since lunchtime.

"I would have suggested we meet in my suite," he commented, "but I figured you'd prefer neutral territory."

Jen nodded. She needed to make something clear right away. "My loyalties are with Beth."

"Of course." Jonah took a deep breath. "What's she up to?"

"She started a job as a music therapist in Sydney a month ago." Jen left location details general. No doubt Jonah could track Beth down if he wanted to, but it didn't hurt to protect her friend's privacy. Which reminded her... "How did you discover where I worked?"

"When Beth and I met up again at the Bachelor and Spinster Ball she mentioned you were heading home to a job here." Jonah glanced around their opulent surroundings. "I couldn't pass up the chance to find out how she's doing."

The concern in his voice answered one question. He still loved Beth.

"She's doing great," Jen reassured him. "That weekend was a turning point for the better. Partly down to you, I think." That's why she'd agreed to this drink.

"I miss her every damn day," he blurted. "Three months with no contact, it's tough." His eyes met Jen's, full of anguish. "I didn't expect waiting to be so hard."

Jen knew Jonah and Beth had never discussed him waiting for her—Beth would never ask that of him—but Jen wasn't surprised that this man was prepared to wait for her friend anyway. Beth was special.

Jen steeled herself to play devil's advocate. "What if she's never ready? Would waiting have been a waste of time for you? I'm sure you've got plenty of other offers." Never again should Beth have to question a man's commitment.

Jonah's mouth tightened. "I'm not her cheating ex-husband."

The bartender brought the drinks and Jonah fell silent while he placed them on the glass table.

Seeing the bar was temporarily empty, Jen pulled out the chair beside her. "Join us a minute," she invited their server. "I think you'll have something to offer."

When Jonah blinked, she smiled mischievously. "This is Logan. We met the same weekend at the Bachelor and Spinster Ball."

"When you were wearing a cow suit?" Smiling, Jonah shook Logan's hand. "Beth mentioned it at the time."

"I was one of the security guards," Logan explained, taking a seat. His fingers threaded through Jen's and she wondered if she'd ever stop being thrilled by the casual possessiveness of his touch. Straight-faced, he added, "Our paths kept mysteriously crossing."

Jonah sipped his craft beer. "Drunken wranglers. Attractive bovine. Yeah, I can see how that might happen." Clearly, Logan's fellow Australian shared his sly humor. Jonah checked the label of the Aotearoa pale ale. "Nice brew," he said to Logan. "So, tell me how you two overcame the species barrier."

As Logan filled him in, Jonah's gaze sharpened. "You went after the girl… You didn't let her get away."

"Our situations are different," Logan said. He glanced at Jen, his dark-blue eyes alight with laughter. "How do I put this diplomatically?"

She grinned. "Don't bother, lover." She looked at Jonah. "I needed saving from myself," she explained, then sobered. "But Beth needs to remember who she is before she makes another commitment."

Jonah's thoughtful gaze traveled between her and Logan. "There are extra pressures on a long distance relationship… Has it been worth it?"

"Hell, no," said Logan, grinning at Jen. They'd played this game before. She'd asked the same question obsessively for the first month, determined to give him an out if he wanted it. Her heart started to pound. "We're in a public pl—" Logan kissed her. He kissed her as though it was the first time he was giving her his heart. How did he do that? Devastate and woo her... Every Single Time.

Jonah grinned. "Dumb question."

Jen lectured Logan on appropriate behavior in front of strangers, while Jonah smirked over his beer. But she didn't release her lover's hand until a customer came in. Attempting to look penitent—and failing—Logan stood to return to the bar. "Good luck," he shook hands with Jonah. "I hope it works out."

"Me too."

When he'd left, Jen tried to harness her happy grin— also a fail.

"And Beth said *you* were the cynic," Jonah teased.

"When you've met the right person," she admitted, "no one else will do."

"No one else will do," he repeated softly. They looked at each other a long moment.

"Here's what I've recently learned about love," she said. "If you want someone to meet your deepest needs you have to be brave enough to meet theirs. I can't promise you a happy ending with Beth. I can only tell you how to deserve one. Give her the time she needs."

"Hurry up and wait." He grimaced. "I knew that. I just needed to be reminded by someone else who loves her." He leaned across the table and hugged her. "Damn you, Jen."

"You're welcome." She raised her glass. "To love."

He tapped it with her beer bottle. "To love."

When Jonah left to unpack fifteen minutes later, Jen stayed to wait for Logan who was swapping shifts. Their tiny apartment was only a few blocks from the hotel and she kept the conversation casual until they stepped inside the door. But the moment it closed she wrapped her arms around Logan.

"I'm so lucky," she said through a tight throat. "I'm

the luckiest woman in the world." Though Ellie might contest that.

"Wow, and this after an hour with a country rock god. I'm flattered." He stroked her back, instinctively understanding why she needed comfort. "You think they'll make it?"

"I hope so." Releasing him, Jen reached up and mussed up his hair. It had grown into sexy waves that she refused to let him shear.

"Let me take your mind off it," he murmured, kissing the tip of her nose. "After I've taken off my work clothes and had a shower." He wore dark pants and a dark shirt that smelled faintly of beer. "Stay in yours, though." His hands curved over her butt in the pencil skirt. "The corporate power suit is a major turn-on."

"You just love a girl in uniform," she teased.

"This girl I do." Pinching her ass, he disappeared into the bathroom.

Jen glanced at Clarabelle as she walked into the bedroom. "Hey honey, we're home, and no, I haven't told him yet. Still working up to it." Their 'cowhide' rug lay on the floor, her eyes permanently rolled upward.

Kicking off her heels, Jen removed her jewelry and unfastened a couple of buttons to entice her man with some cleavage. Then she plumped up the pillows and settled on the bed.

For the initial six weeks of their relationship they'd snatched a long weekend here, a mid-week break there. It wasn't enough. During an Auckland stay, Logan had talked his way into a job at the hotel bar—which paid expenses and left his retirement check intact—and moved into the tiny studio apartment Jen had taken on a short lease. He'd accommodated his life to her responsibilities and she appreciated it.

Clarabelle was still staring, Jen frowned at her. "Sheesh, will you quit with the nagging? Fine, I'll tell him now."

"Tell me what now?" Logan walked into the

bedroom, rubbing his hair dry with a towel. Another towel was slung low around his hips. Jen took a moment to appreciate the vision before answering.

"The conference coordinator I'm covering for isn't coming back. The GM offered me a permanent position."

"Okay," said Logan. She watched him process the implications as he finished toweling his hair. One of the many qualities she loved about this man was his calmness under pressure.

These past weeks had been the happiest of Jen's life; she and the Terminator sharing a fifty square meter space. Seeing him in the small kitchen brewing their morning coffee was her favorite way to start the day.

Maybe it was Logan's army training, maybe it was his character but he could make a home anywhere. Jen hadn't realized how much she'd needed one. *No,* she thought. *How much I needed some*one *to call my own.*

"Before you say anything" she said. "I turned it down."

"You don't have to." Logan wiped away the last drops of water on his torso and arms. "We'll make it work."

Jen's suggestion that he consider a career in Search and Rescue had taken root and Logan had enrolled in specialist training courses to supplement his already impressive CV. In a couple of weeks, he started classes in Canberra and Jen had planned to take a three month break—her first in five years—and go with him, the two of them taking road-trips into the wilderness around his studies.

"Yes," she said. "I do have to turn it down. We do what's best for us, now, not just me. And there's more to my life—more to *me*—than work. Which is not to say, I won't still out-earn your altruistic butt while you're busy saving people every day."

Laughing, Logan tossed the towel aside. "I'm counting on it."

"I want more spontaneity in my life, some fun and adventure," she said as he walked toward the bed. "But most of all, I want to be with you. We belong together."

He stopped at the end of the bed, his dark-blue eyes serious. "I love you," he said. "You are my One, my soulmate, my heart."

Jen blinked away tears. "I might have to marry you, you know that don't you?"

Removing the second towel around his hips, Logan dropped it over Clarabelle's eyes and stood there, naked and magnificent. "I don't think she's old enough for the X-rated convincing I'm about to do to you," he explained.

With a happy sigh, Jen put her hands behind her head and leaned back against the pillows. "I do love your mad skills." She surveyed the prime beef on the hoof standing in front of her and grinned. "So…woo me."

END

Thanks for reading WOO ME.* I appreciate *all* reviews on Goodreads or your favorite retailer, whether negative or positive. For news on upcoming releases you can join my mailing list by visiting www.karinabliss.com or by sending an email to: karina@karinabliss.com with the subject line: Newsletter.

About the Author

New Zealander Karina Bliss's debut, *Mr Imperfect*, won a ***Romantic Book of the Year*** award in Australia, the first of eleven books published through Harlequin SuperRomance. In January 2015, she published *Rise* – the first of her new ***Rock Solid series***, about the (rising, falling and rising) fortunes of a rock band.

Rise continues the story of Zander Freedman, who first appeared as a villain in ***What the Librarian Did*** – a book that made *Dear Author's Best of the Year* list in 2010. Two of Karina's books have also featured in *Sizzling Book Chats* at *SmartBitchesTrashyBooks* and as *Desert Island Keepers* at *likesbooks.com*.

Karina lives on the sunny Hibiscus Coast with her family.

For more information on the author visit www.karinabliss.com

Beth Walker hasn't just been burned by her philandering country music star ex, she's been barbecued to a crisp.

Coming home to Australia and into the arms of her best friends is exactly the balm she needs. Cocktails and laughter at an Outback Bachelor and Spinster Ball seem like the perfect distraction.

Until she bumps into the last person she wants seeing her heartsick and pathetic—Jonah Masters, rising country music star and witness to the failure of her marriage. If only she'd met Jonah first. Now she's broken and won't ask him to wait until she heals.

Jonah can't believe he and Beth are finally standing under the same stars.

The connection they shared on the road years ago has haunted him but he wasn't going to pursue a married woman. Now she's free, and Jonah can't refuse the one night Beth impulsively offers.

Can he convince the woman he's always loved that he'll wait—however long it takes—for her trust?

EXCERPT

BETH STOPPED IN HER TRACKS when she realized why everyone was acting so strangely—a black SUV was parked to one side of the catering tent, the crowd forming a semi-circle around it.

Four men were collecting various pieces of musical equipment from the rear of the vehicle. She recognized the blonde-haired giant with the guitar case first, then the tall, broad-shouldered man standing next to him turned around, a second guitar case in his hand, and four years blew away like dust as she saw his familiar face.

Jonah.

Jonah, with his gorgeous, open smile and warm, cognac eyes. A smile curved her mouth as she took in his worn jeans, wrinkled black shirt and ruffled russet-brown hair. He looked exactly the same. *Exactly.*

The memory of what their short friendship had once meant to her was so strong, the pleasure she felt at seeing him again so intense, she actually took a step forward, his name on her lips. Then all the reasons he was the absolute last person she wanted to see crashed down on her.

The tacit warning he'd issued, the scene he'd witnessed between her and Troy…

She started to backtrack, desperate to duck out of sight before he saw her. Then he glanced over the crowd, and *of course* his gaze found hers, because her life totally sucked right now. Despite everything—the years since they'd seen each other, the shortness of her stupid new haircut, the sheer improbability of the two of them being at this obscure event in the middle of nowhere—his face lit with recognition.

"Beth," he said, starting toward her.

Hell, no.

No way was she doing this. Not in this lifetime. Beth ducked back between the two men she'd just slipped past, her heart beating a frantic tattoo against her breastbone.

"Beth."

Damn. He was following her. She broke into a jog, dodging her way around a large group of revelers and practically diving head-first into the throng inside the pavilion. Wriggling like a minnow, she slipped between gaps and ducked under elbows and squeezed past backsides. She only stopped when she was entrenched in the thick crowd around the bar, well hidden from anyone who might have come after her. Standing with her face in someone's armpit, she closed her eyes and sent up a prayer of thanks to the universe.

Thank God she didn't have to look Jonah in the eye and deal with his pity. Thank. God.

Her heart still banging against her chest, she made her way more slowly toward the side entrance. Just in case Jonah was still searching for her out the front.

At least the crowd's awestruck reaction made sense now. Even in rural Australia, people responded like catnip to fame, and Jonah Masters and the Rowdy Boys had it in spades. Ever since their third album had gone platinum two years ago, they'd become the hottest thing in country music, selling out every gig on a multi-state tour across the U.S. before coming home to Australia and sending fans into a frenzy usually reserved for teen idols like Bieber and Perry.

Which begged the question: what the hell were they doing at the Dubbo Bachelor and Spinster Ball? With their instruments, no less?

The crowd was locked solid near the side entrance and it took her a while to break through to the outdoors again. She heaved a sigh of relief once she could actually start walking at a normal pace. Crisis averted. Time to escape from here and get on with her brooding for the evening. The great thing was, she could now add Jonah to her list of Things to Overthink. That ought to kill at least a good hour or two before she moved onto general regret that she'd ever met Troy Banks and been stupid enough to fall for him.

She'd just cleared the line of portable toilets marching along one side of the pavilion when a warm hand gripped her upper arm.

"Beth."

Jonah stepped in front of her, blocking her escape, and she had to dig her heels in to avoid plowing into his chest.

"Shit," she said under her breath. She couldn't believe he'd outflanked her. But he'd always been good at guessing what was on her mind.

"Good to see you, too," he said. Despite his words, his eyes were warm, not condemning, and he gave her arm a little squeeze before releasing her.

He felt sorry for her. The knowledge sent heat rushing into her face.

"What are you even doing here?" she asked.

"Doing a favor for a mate. The main act dropped out at the last minute, and the guys and I were at a loose end, kicking around in Sydney, when we got the mayday call." His gaze was running over her face, as though he was relearning what she looked like.

She lifted a self-conscious hand to her hair before she could stop herself.

"What are *you* doing here?" he asked.

"A couple of my oldest friends wanted to come. It's kind of a reunion type thing."

"Are these the friends you went to boarding school with?"

She blinked, stunned that he'd remembered such a small, insignificant detail mentioned casually in a conversation they'd shared more than *four years ago.*

"That's right. Ellie and Jen."

People were starting to recognize Jonah, stopping to

stare or pulling out their phones to take picture to prove they'd really run into *the* Jonah Masters. Any second now they'd be in the center of a full-fledged crowd. After years of being married to a successful musician, the dynamic was so familiar, it gave Beth chills. This was what fame did to your life—you couldn't even have a conversation with an old friend in public.

"You should go," she said.

He glanced at the gathering crowd.

"Have a drink with me after the gig," he asked when his focus returned to her face.

"I can't." The words popped out of her mouth before she'd had a chance to formulate a decent excuse to cover her reluctance.

"Why not?"

"I'm not... I'm not great company right now," she said lamely.

It was the truth, but it wasn't the full truth. She didn't want to be the object of his pity. It was galling enough that he'd played witness to her stupendous gullibility all those years ago. "Let me be the judge of that," he said.

She started to shake her head, but he moved a step closer, his golden eyes looking straight into hers as he rested a hand on her shoulder.

"I've been thinking about you," he said, his voice low and slightly rough. "Ever since I heard."

She laughed, the sound bitter and sharp. "You're not the only one. At one stage the *Enquirer* was offering up to $20,000 for a photograph of me post-split."

He cocked his head slightly, his eyes narrowed as he studied her.

"It's just a drink, Beth. Nothing to be afraid of."

"I know that," she said, too quickly. "I'm not afraid."

"Then meet me after the set."

He smiled then, and she blinked, momentarily dazzled by the sheer loveliness of the man. He was so *warm*. There was no other way to describe it. The color of his hair and eyes, the raw, electric energy that seemed to emanate from his big body, the way he looked at her as though she was the only consideration in his world right now.

"All right," she said, because some stupid part of her wanted to, and because she knew he wouldn't give up easily and she didn't have it in her to fight both herself and him right now.

Want more? Visit: www.sarahmayberry.com

Feisty, fearless Ellie McFarlane has tried *forever* to get cattle station manager, Rick Drummond, to notice she's not another cowhand. So when her gal pals talk her into glamming up for an Outback Bachelor and Spinster ball she's eager to prove she's all woman, all the time, and leave her boneheaded cowboy eating dust.

Sexy wrangler Rick is crazy about Ellie just as she is but her father—his *boss*—told him long ago that his daughter was off limits. Even though she's all grown up now, Rick still feels it's his job is to protect her, not seduce her. Plus, he's finally got an opportunity to buy back his family farm which means moving far away.

Ellie's transformation from Cinder-Ellie to belle of the ball has Rick's jaw dropping—and all the other cowboys falling at her feet. Ellie tries to revel in her new-found sex-pot status but without Rick it's a hollow victory. Has Rick left it too late to claim the only woman he'll ever truly love….

EXCERPT

ELLIE GAZED GLUMLY INTO HER bedroom closet looking for a suitable dress to wear to the Bachelor Ball. She was a cowgirl, not a girly girl, so there wasn't a lot on offer. "My old pink chiffon will have to do."

Jen and Beth lounged on the bed, margaritas in hand. Their reunion weekend was off to a flying start. Now Ellie had to live up to her friends' dare to glam up for the ball.

"No way. I'm going to burn the chiffon." Jen jumped up, ripped the dress off the hanger and threw it in a corner. "Never fear, I have the perfect dress for you."

She dragged her suitcase onto Ellie's bed and flipped it open. Delicately, she lifted out a floor-length dress in ivory silk with pencil-thin black horizontal lines. It was a halter top with black spaghetti straps and a deep V-necked bodice. There was absolutely no back to it.

"I can't wear that!" Ellie gulped at her margarita. "I'd be practically naked."

"Try it on," Beth urged. "It'll look brilliant on you."

Suddenly the reality of her wearing this glamorous dress hit Ellie with the force of three margaritas. "It's too sexy for me. Do you have something tamer?"

Boot heels sounded on the wooden planks of the veranda. Rick rested his elbows on the window ledge and peered in, the light curtains billowing around his broad shoulders. His dark blond hair framed a ruggedly handsome face. "From all the laughing I heard earlier, you girls sound as if you're having fun. Hey, Beth, Jen. Haven't seen you two in ages."

"Rick." Beth went over to give him a hug. "Don't you ever stop working?"

"Not when there are chores to be done. Careful you don't blow away in the next breeze, girl."

"My feet are firmly planted on the ground," Beth, claimed, swaying lightly.

He released Beth and turned to hug Jen, immaculate in designer wear. "You gals want to help me and Norm bring home the weaner calves?"

Jen punched his shoulder. "When have you ever needed help with that?"

Ellie smiled affectionately as her friends bantered with Rick. It meant a lot to her that Jen and Beth liked Rick even though they privately referred to him as her bone-headed cowboy for not seeing Ellie as anything more than a kid sister or a cowhand.

Rick pushed his hat back on his head. "Been a long time since the three Musketeers have been together. You two come to get the country girl in trouble again?"

"Absolutely," Jen said.

"It's our duty," Beth added solemnly.

Rick nodded at the cow suit draped over a chair. "Are you wearing that to the ball again, Ellie?"

"No, Jen is."

"What are you going as?" he asked her.

"A woman," she said loftily. "So there."

"A woman," he repeated with a faint note of incredulity. His blue eyes crinkled.

Ellie's cheeks burned. In her torn cut-offs and bare feet she'd never felt more like a farm girl. Which was fine because that's who she was. But was it too much to ask that just once, just one friggin' time, Rick would acknowledge she was also an adult female and sexually desirable?

"She's going to hook up with the hottest guy at the ball," Beth said.

"They'll be lining up to dance with her." Jen stabbed a finger at him. "Just you wait and see how sexy she looks."

"I'm not going to the ball this year. I've got business to attend to." Then he laughed and shook his head. "A woman. Ellie, you are so nuts if you think—"

"Don't you have a barn to muck out?" Ellie snapped and started to close the window. Quickly he retracted his head before the sash came down on his neck. She whisked the curtains closed, plunging the room into an orange-tinted haze that matched the outrage burning inside her.

"That does it." She absolutely refused to pine after him another second. Peeling her tank top over her head she tossed it aside and dropped her shorts in a puddle on the floor. "Let's do this. Make me a sex bomb."

"Atta girl. Take your bra off, too," Jen instructed, bringing the dress to her.

"How will the dress stay on my boobs?" Ellie eyed the skinny halter top warily as she removed her sensible cotton bra. "I'll wobble all over the place."

"With those firm puppies? No way," Beth said. She and Jen lowered the dress over Ellie's head.

"I've got special tape," Jen added. "Don't worry, there'll be no wardrobe malfunctions."

Ellie let the silky fabric slide over her near-naked body and shimmied to settle it over her hips. The dress felt super soft against her skin and swung with her slightest movement. Wow. She felt like Cinderella. Only instead of ugly step-sisters she was in the company of the kindest, most beautiful, generous friends ever.

"You guys are the best," she said, overcome by sentiment and tequila. "I mean it. You're both awesome to do this for me."

Beth gave her a hug and spun her around. "Look in the mirror. Then you'll see what awesome is."

Ellie blinked at the image of herself reflected in the full length mirror on the back of her closet door. She hardly recognized the sexy woman staring back at her. Above her waist, more flesh seemed to be exposed than was covered. "I can't wear this. I'll get arrested."

"You'll get laid, is what you'll get." Jen high-fived Beth. "You're going to be a sex goddess."

"We'll do your hair, give you a manicure and

pedicure," Beth went on happily.

Ellie listened in a daze. In this dress, it was easy to imagine she could be the kind of woman Rick was attracted to. Feminine. Sexy. Sultry.

Then the sound of his mocking chuckle came back to her, making her ears heat. Nope, she wasn't trying to attract him. She was getting over him.

"Bring it on," she said. "I am so going to do this."

The next morning Rick set off on the road south to his family's old sheep station he was looking at to buy while Ellie and her friends slept off the margaritas. Ellie's words still rang in his ears. *I'm going as a woman.*

Of course she was a woman. Why did she even need to say it? Beneath her jeans and T-shirt she had amazing breasts and real hips, as he well knew from swimming in the dam with her on hot summer days. And the way she'd said it, as if she had something to prove... A joke, because any fool could see she was all woman, all the time.

The idea that guys didn't know she was hot had made him laugh out loud. But now that he thought about it, maybe that hadn't been the best reaction. She'd seemed pretty pissed when she almost slammed his head in the window.

Ellie's going to hook up with the hottest guy at the ball.

Rick thumped the steering wheel with his fist. Jen and Beth were good friends to Ellie and always supportive but they were more worldly than her, more used to fending off unwanted advances. Of course, in the years she'd spent in America, Ellie had undoubtedly gained experience with men.

I've had me a cowboy or three...

Jealous, him? No, of course not. She was going to hook up with some guy permanently one day. She was too great a girl not to. But whoever she chose had to be good enough for her. If such a man existed.

To distract himself he switched radio stations, happening to land on a local station advertising the Dubbo Bachelor and Spinster Ball. Live music, dancing, open bar from 7:00 pm., barbecue dinner and breakfast...

She's going to be the hottest girl there.

Ellie was pretty, no question. She had a smile that could light up the outback sky and eyes that sparkled like the mossy creek on a sunny day. But hot? She was more the girl-next-door type. That didn't mean she wasn't sexy. She was, but in a good way rather than a manufactured kind of way. He hoped Jen and Beth didn't tart her up too much and spoil her sweet looks. Guys might get the wrong idea about her.

The sun rose higher as the road descended out of the high country into the flat, dry plains of central New South Wales. The farms were larger down here; they had to be to provide enough pasture for grazing. Sheep were more plentiful than cattle because they were more adaptable to the dry conditions.

Nothing wrong with sheep, he told himself, except that he preferred working with cattle. But his dad had lost his shirt doing that. He was nervous, he realized, going back to the old place. He hadn't been there since he and his mom and his sister had loaded all their belongings into a U-Haul and left, beaten and broken. He wanted to honor his father's death, and reclaim his birthright. But there were bad memories there. Sad memories. Was he making a mistake, trying to buy it back?

Driving through the outskirts of Dubbo he passed the showgrounds where temporary fencing had been erected to enclose it. Crews were working on a pavilion with plywood flooring laid directly on the grass to become the dance floor. In the surrounding area tents were being set up for food and beverages. Semi-trailers lined a side road for the catering and the band. He'd been to enough similar events in his time to recognize this as the site of the Bachelor and Spinster Ball.

Ellie would be fine, wouldn't she? Her friends might be hyping her up for a raunchy weekend, but when it came to brass tacks they would look out for her. Something was up with all three of them, though. Jen and Beth had both seemed brittle last night at dinner, Jen's laughter too forced, Beth too quiet. Ellie had acted wild, as if ready to lash out and do something crazy. He wasn't sure he liked the idea of these three women throwing caution to the wind. They egged each other on when they got together.

He had no doubt Ellie's friends intended to pour her into a sexy dress. He shifted in his seat as his pants got a little tighter thinking about her half-naked. He groaned. What was wrong with him? This was Ellie, his boss's daughter. They didn't have that kind of relationship.

Kip put a paw on his leg, his head cocked questioningly. Rick ruffled his ears. "I'm okay, boy. I'll buy my property, get my ass away from Coolibah and forget about Ellie. It's the right thing to do."

So why did it feel so wrong?

Want more? Visit: www.joankilby.com

RISE—The redemption story of a rock star going straight(er) through the love of a good(ish) woman

"You have the ability to make controversial characters sympathetic. Maybe I just want to be understood."

Acclaimed literary biographer Elizabeth Winston writes about long-dead heroes.

So bad-boy rock icon Zander Freedman couldn't possibly tempt her to write his memoir.

Except the man is a mass of fascinating contradictions—manipulative, honest, gifted, charismatic and morally ambiguous.

In short, everything she seeks in a biography subject.

When in her life will she get another chance to work with a living legend? But saying yes to one temptation soon leads to another.

Suddenly she's having heated fantasies about her subject, fantasies this blue-eyed devil is only too willing to stoke.

She thought self-control was in her DNA; after all, she grew up a minister's daughter.

She thought wrong.

Outside your comfort zone is the only place worth living…

Rock star Zander Freedman has been an outlier—many would say an outcast—for most of his life.

But there's no disaster he can't overcome, from the breakup of his band to the inevitable damage to his reputation.

His Resurrection Tour is shaping up to be his greatest triumph—if his golden voice holds out.

Contracting a respected biographer is simply about creating more buzz. Elizabeth's integrity is the key to consolidating his legacy as one of rock's greats.

All the damn woman has to do is write down what he tells her. Not force him to think.

Or encourage the good guy struggling to get out.

And certainly not make him fall in love for the first time in his life.

Turns out he is scared of something: being known.

Read excerpt on www.karinabliss.com